THE GUARDIANS

THE SANDMAN AND THE WAR OF DREAMS

Sanderson Mansnoozie
SEXTANS

THE GUARDIANS

THE SANDMAN AND THE WAR OF DREAMS

WILLIAM JOYCE

atheneum

A Caitlyn Dlouhy Book

ATHENEUM BOOKS FOR YOUNG READERS

NEW YORK • LONDON • TORONTO • SYDNEY • NEW DELHI

Atheneum Books for Young Readers
An imprint of Simon & Schuster Children's Publishing Division
1230 Avenue of the Americas, New York, New York 10020

Also available in an Atheneum Books for Young Readers hardcover edition
Book design by Lauren Rille
The text for this book was set in Adobe Jenson Pro.
The illustrations for this book were rendered in a combination of charcoal, graphite, and digital media.
Manufactured in the United States of America
0718 MTN
First Atheneum Books for Young Readers paperback edition September 2018
10 9 8 7 6 5 4 3 2 1
The Library of Congress has cataloged the hardcover edition as follows:
Joyce, William, 1957– author, illustrator.
The Sandman and the war of dreams / William Joyce. — 1st ed.
p. cm. — (The Guardians)
Summary: When Pitch and Katherine go missing, the Man in the Moon recruits the sleepy but clever Sandman to aid the Guardians' cause in an adventure that finds them struggling to convince their new member to accept a more optimistic perspective.
ISBN 978-1-4424-3054-9 (hc)
ISBN 978-1-4424-3055-6 (pbk)
ISBN 978-1-4424-8146-6 (eBook)
[1. Sandman (Legendary character)—Juvenile fiction. 2. Dreams—Juvenile fiction. 3. Sleep—Juvenile fiction. 4. Sandman—Fiction. 5. Dreams—Fiction. 6. Sleep—Fiction. 7. Fantasy.]
PZ7.J857 Sam 2013
[Fic]—dc23 2013404170

To my Dream Captains:

George Melies, Jean Cocteau,

and

George Auric

Contents

Mother Nature

The Newest Guardian
Sandman

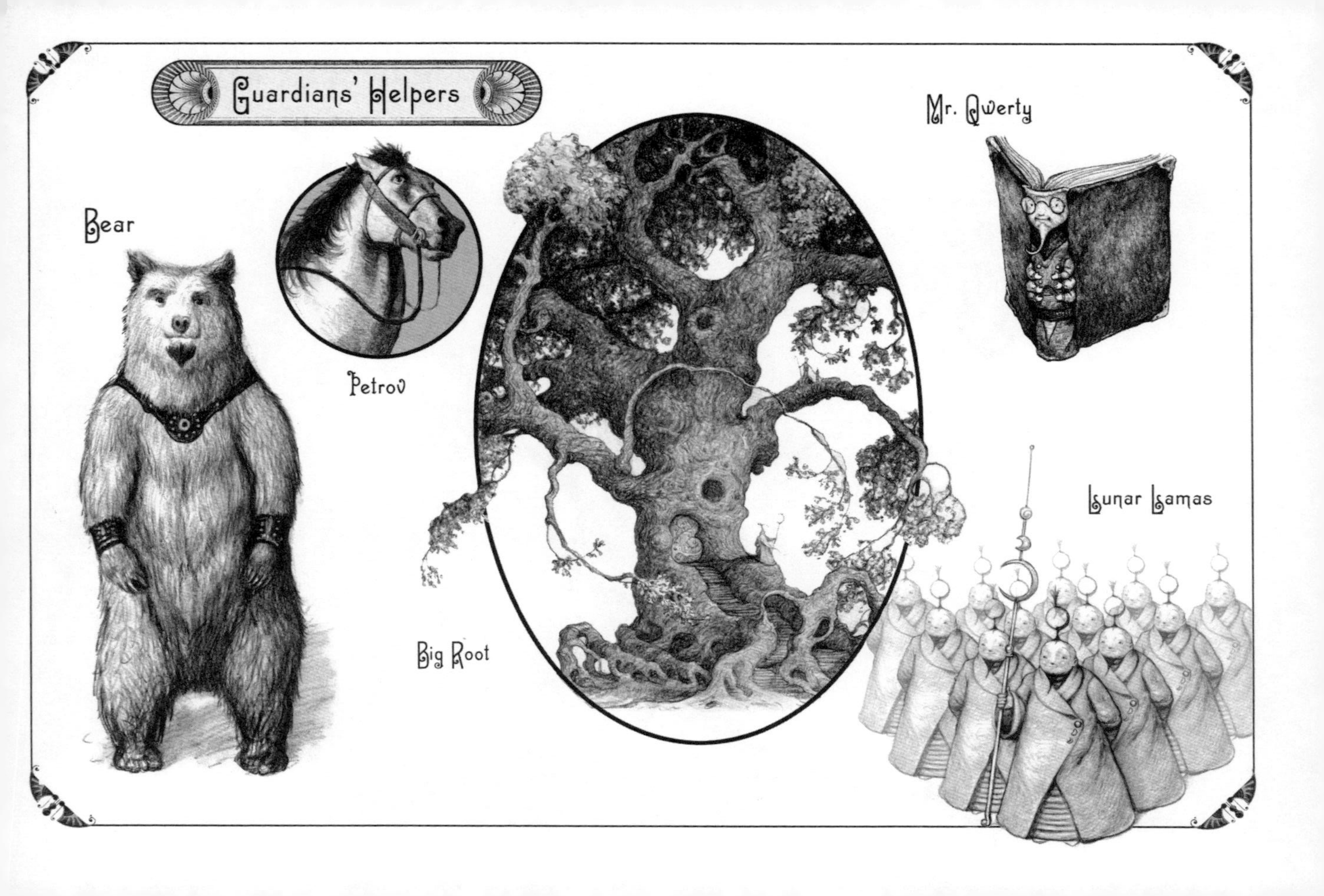
Guardians' Helpers
Bear
Petrov
Big Root
Mr. Qwerty
Lunar Lamas

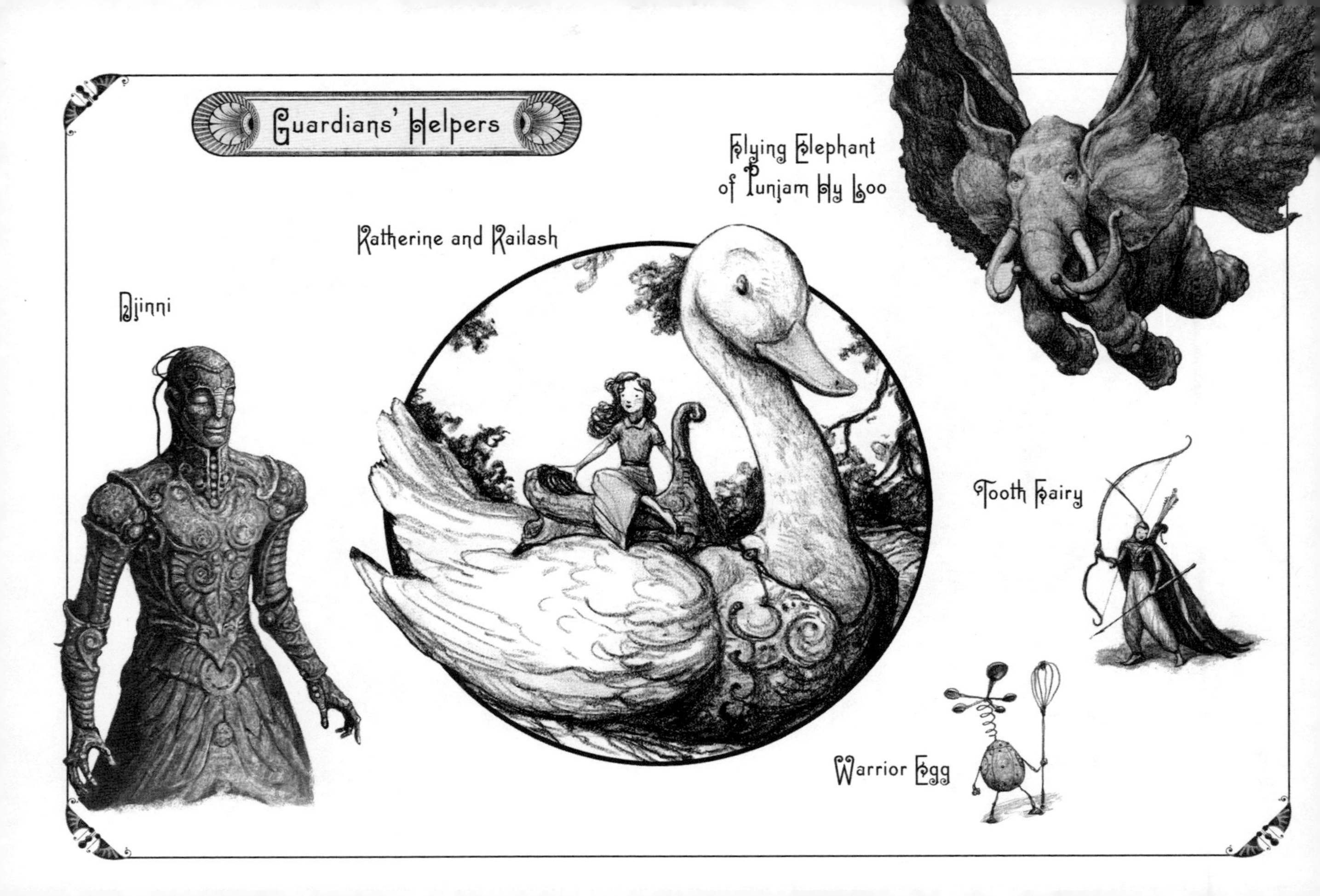
Guardians' Helpers
Flying Elephant
of Punjam Hy Loo
Katherine and Kailash
Djinni
Tooth Fairy
Warrior Egg

The Villains
Pitch
the Nightmare King
Fearlings
The Dream Pirate
Pitch's Galleon
A Nightmare Man

Guardians
Queen Toothiana
North
Ombric
Katherine
and
Nightlight
Bunnymund

CHAPTER ONE

The Dreams That Stuff Is Made Of

TIME PASSES STRANGELY WHEN you are sleeping. You can close your eyes when it is night, then open them again and see morning. Yet the hours that went by seemed no longer than the drifting journey of a leaf in a soft breeze.

Strange, wondrous, and terrible adventures are the norm in dreams. Uncharted lands come and go. Dream epics play out. Wars are fought and won. Loved ones are lost or found. Entirely different lives are lived as we sleep. And then we awake, with disappointment or relief, as if nothing at all had happened.

But sometimes things do happen.

In the waking world, the Guardians had lost one of their own to a powerful entity known as Mother Nature.

But an odd little man had been sleeping for more days and nights than any calendar could count. The snoozing fellow was the color of golden sand—indeed, he seemed to be made of the stuff. And his unruly hair twirled and twisted as he slept. He rested in the dune-covered center of a tiny star-shaped island that was nearly impossible for humans to find, for it was not originally from the Earth. The island was not connected to anything; no landmass beneath the ocean anchored it in place. As such, it was the only island on our planet that truly floated atop the water. Because of this, it drifted. In June it might be in the Pacific Ocean, and by July it might be off the coast of Madagascar, its whereabouts known only to the Moon and the stars.

Which was fitting, for this island had once *been* a star. It had been saved by the leader of the Guardians, Tsar Lunar, or as we call him, the "Man in the Moon." But that was ages ago.

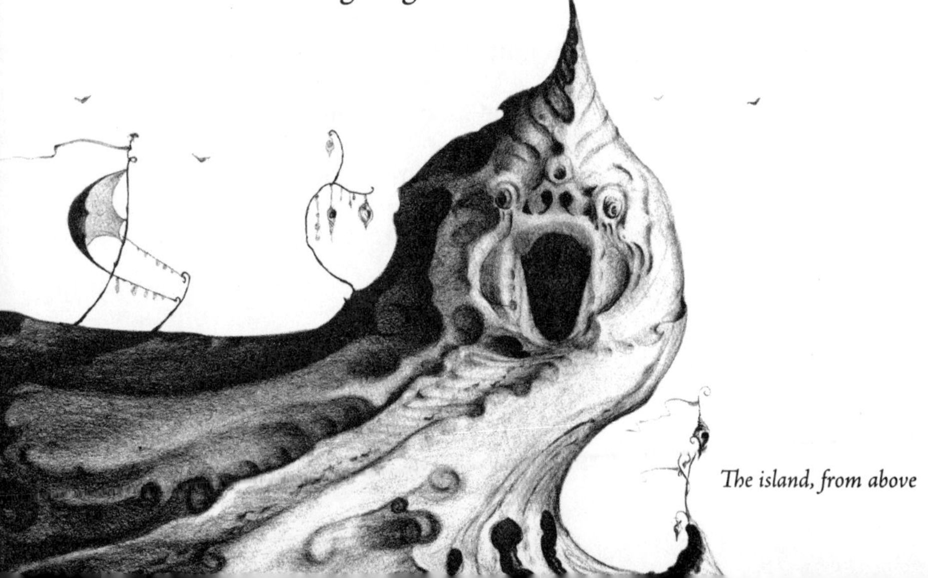

The island, from above

On *this* most auspicious night, Tsar Lunar called upon the small and harmless-looking fellow who softly snored among the island's magic sands.

But how should one awaken a man from the past? A man who had traveled oceans of time and space. A steadfast fellow who had piloted the fastest shooting star in the heavens. A hero of ten thousand battles against Pitch, the Nightmare King. This smallish warrior had once been the most valiant granter of wishes the cosmos had ever known. How does one wake a man who has not opened his eyes since the great ancient days of the Golden Age?

As with most things, the answer was simple.

The Man in the Moon sent a moonbeam messenger with a single whispered request: "I wish that you would help. Your powers are needed."

In an instant the little man's eyes opened. The

centuries of sleep fell away. There he stood, tall as he could: Sanderson Mansnoozie. The Man in the Moon then proceeded to relay his full message. Sanderson Mansnoozie listened intently.

So very much had happened while he had slept.

Pitch had returned and was threatening the galaxies again. But Sanderson Mansnoozie's long sleep had been most productive. He was now more powerful than he had ever been: He had power over the world of dreams. In fact, every grain of sand on his island now contained a dream—one dream from each night of his nearly endless sleep, and all of them good dreams, strong enough to fight any nightmare.

When the Man in the Moon finished, Sanderson Mansnoozie, with a wave of his hands, brought his island to life. Its sands swirled around him, and the island transformed into a cloud that swept him up from the sea and into the sky.

With moonbeams to guide him, he sailed the golden cloud toward his mission: to aide the Guardians. To save and rescue a girl named Katherine. And to stop Pitch forever.

This "Sandman" was ready to seek out his ancient enemy and oldest friends. He was ready to face whatever dangers lay ahead.

And there were many.

Chapter Two

A Return to Where Things Started

For the Guardians and their allies, it had been a hectic and miserable trip from Queen Toothiana's mountain palace in Punjam Hy Loo. After the horror of seeing their Katherine, and Pitch, abducted by Mother Nature's cyclone, the Guardians had decided they should return to the village of Santoff Claussen. Santoff Claussen was the place where magic, goodness, and bravery were tended and protected. It was where they had been linked and where their new lives as Guardians had been born. It was a place that felt like home.

But the Guardians felt lost and broken. They could not sense Katherine. Where she might be. If she was in peril or safe.

Home. They needed that feeling of "home"; the safety and warmth, the dreamlike comforts that are "home."

E. Aster Bunnymund was the last of the giant rabbits of the Pookan Brotherhood, and while he had been to Santoff Claussen only a few times, he had found his first friends in the enchanted village.

Nicholas St. North had been the greatest thief in all of Russia and had once tried to rob Santoff Claussen of its treasures. But the kindness he had found there had changed his brigand's heart, and now he was a hero of unparalleled skill and valor.

For Toothiana, Queen of the Tooth Fairy Armies, this would be her first real visit. She had heard from her many animal friends that the village was a haven of kindness and respect for all living creatures. She already felt a great kinship with any who came from Santoff Claussen.

Ombric Shalazar ached to return to the village he had founded. This most ancient and wise of wizards hoped that by going back to Santoff Claussen, the Guardians would heal from their battles with Pitch. Such a cunning and relentless villain was this Nightmare King! Three times now the Guardians had defeated him. And three times he had returned, with deeply devious plans that had tested them beyond what they thought they could ever do. They were weary and heartsick. But Ombric . . . Ombric was close to collapse. His weariness was now equal to his wisdom, and he feared that perhaps he was losing the delicate balance that kept him ready for any fight.

Going home must mend me, he thought. He hoped it would steady them all, give them a chance to regroup, gather their strength, and re-sharpen their wits. They would need to if they stood any chance of finding Katherine.

This lost girl may have been the youngest of their troop, but in many ways she was its oldest soul. She was orphaned, as all the Guardians had been, and like them, she had found a path out of that sorrow. Unlike them, however, her path was not through daring deeds or the study of magic or the use of miraculous powers. She had been gifted with something almost as rare: an open and eager mind. She had the gift of watching and listening, the gift of taking all the hurts and happenings of others' lives and understanding their purpose.

Katherine's heart and mind would take their

adventures and reimagine them, sometimes exactly as they had occurred or—most miraculously of all—as new stories. She had become the historian of what had happened and what should have happened. No one could tell a story better than Katherine. No one understood what needed to be as well as she. This was a singular and important power in the ranks of the Guardians.

But Nightlight was the most eager of them to be back in Santoff Claussen. He was well named, this quicksilver boy of brightness and unending youth. His pureness of heart could cast away the darkest shadows. Katherine was his best, closest, dearest friend. He had first met her in the village, and their friendship had changed him, made him more of what was best inside his joyful, restless soul. With Katherine at his side, he felt he could light up the world. And he quite likely could. But now she was gone.

And so the remaining Guardians would return, along with all the villagers and children and animals who had joined them on what was intended as a celebratory journey.

It had been a time so full of hope and promise. Peace was coming. A new Golden Age was at hand.

But war and disaster had come instead.

They now boarded Bunnymund's Eggomotive and made the long trek home. As the wondrous locomotive rose from its tunnel and into the village, they immediately sensed an unfamiliar air of worry.

All who had stayed behind in the village came rushing out to greet them.

In front were Petrov, North's uncannily smart stallion, and Bear, the most magnificent of his species to ever walk the forests of Europe. Bear was as gentle as he was powerful. The robot, Djinni, was beside him. This extraordinary metal being, built by North, was capable of untold amazements. Flanking the three were Bunnymund's Warrior Eggs of all sizes, standing at attention. Hovering above them was the Spirit of the Forest, her robes shimmering in unseen winds. Behind them were all the creatures of the forest and the villagers, each smartly dressed in the customary Santoff Claussen attire. Even the beetles and worms wore dapper vests and hats.

And of course Ombric's owls were there as well. These mysterious birds had the ability to absorb knowledge from out of the air, so they knew everything that had happened during this fateful trip of the Guardians. Within Big Root, the massive hollow tree that was the center of the village, the owls had been able to activate the magical screens that hung in Ombric's laboratory.

From the minds of the owls, the screens had projected to everyone in Santoff Claussen the story of what had happened in Punjam Hy Loo. So everyone in the village had seen the meeting of Queen Toothiana and the twisted Monkey King who had allied with Pitch. They had learned of the battle against the monkey army, in which Pitch's long-lost daughter had returned and taken Pitch and Katherine. They knew everything except the one detail the owls did not know. It was the one detail that would put all their minds at ease: Where was Katherine?

As the engine of Bunnymund's Eggomotive stopped and its egg-shaped puffs of smoke cleared, the village and all its citizens came together again.

Cautious hellos and welcomes were exchanged. Parents hugged their children. Old William embraced all his younger Williams. But the joy in this reunion was shadowed. The children who had just returned from the journey broke from their parents' clutches and clustered around Kailash, the Great Himalayan Snow Goose who had been raised by Katherine. The huge bird's graceful neck hung low. The villagers had hoped beyond hope that the Guardians might have an answer as to Katherine's whereabouts, but because they did not, the band of heroes was lowest of all. And when the smallest William raced up to Mr. Qwerty, the former glowworm who'd transformed himself into a magic book in a moment of dire need and whose pages were filled with Katherine's every story—his pages were Katherine's pages; her stories, his stories—Mr.

Qwerty opened himself and showed one blank page after another. His life, without her, was on pause. There were no new stories beyond her first ones—no clue as to where Katherine was or if she was all right.

Chapter Three

In Which We See Many Terrors in the Shadows

Katherine was worried as well. She was straining to hear the volatile discussion between her captors, but it was difficult. She had no idea where she was, but she was certain it was unlike any place she'd ever been. And she'd seen many amazing places: the enchanted forest that surrounded Santoff Claussen. The eerie majesty of Pitch's lair at the Earth's core. The gilded splendor of Bunnymund's underground city, where everything—right down to the doorknobs—was egg-shaped. Queen Toothiana's haunting palace at the highest peak of Punjam Hy Loo.

She assumed this densely wooded place where she was being held must be part of Mother Nature's empire. The ground seemed to be made of an ever-changing mix of earth and water. Oddly, it never became muddy; the elements stayed separate. Spirals of water encircled the trees' roots like miniature moats, and widened and narrowed whenever Katherine moved. Mist and fog spun through the air in delicate patterns. They looked like layer after layer of glistening lace that heaved and rippled in the constant breeze.

The trees were of every size and sat close together. The high canopy of leaves was so thick that almost no direct sunlight filtered through. The few low-hanging branches curled and swayed with the haunting grace of a dancer's arms.

It was these armlike branches that held Katherine

tightly at the base of one particularly massive tree. Every time she pulled against them, their grip intensified. If she tried to take even a single step, the moats around the tree would widen and deepen. The water was black and menacing.

So, for the present, she resigned herself to the fact that she could not break loose, and she instead concentrated on eavesdropping. The mist muffled almost all sound, but she could manage to make out the voices of Pitch and Mother Nature. What she heard fascinated and terrified her.

"You saved me," Pitch was saying, his voice a curious mix of pride and vulnerability.

"No," Mother Nature replied dismissively. "It was the girl who saved you. The one who *you* would make your Darkling Princess."

Katherine knew they were talking about her. She

had taken pity on Pitch and stopped the Guardians from killing him. But there was a hardness in Mother Nature's voice that made Katherine uneasy.

"Had you forgotten me?" Mother Nature demanded. "Your own daughter!"

Katherine was amazed that this magnificent woman of the elements was Pitch's long-lost child.

The breeze began to strengthen. The air grew considerably colder. Katherine could now see her breath.

"No!" Katherine heard Pitch cry out. "I never for a moment forgot you."

"Then why did you not come for me?" Mother Nature asked with a chilling calm.

"I tried! I tried. . . . For so long, I tried—" Pitch's voice broke off in anguish.

Mother Nature's silence after this pleading admission was telling.

The air became wintery. The lacy mist froze into sheets of stiffened frost. Katherine realized what was happening. As Mother Nature's voice grew colder, so did the air around her.

"You failed me, Father," she said, her voice low and dangerous. "I was lost. I had nothing but my rage at you to feed me. I came to your aid only out of . . . curiosity. To see how a once-great man could become so fallen and low."

It began to snow furiously. Katherine was freezing. She could now faintly see Pitch crawling toward her, as if in agony. Mother Nature walked behind him, calmly and regally.

"You will receive only indifference from me, Father. I will neither hinder nor help you," she was saying. "I demand only one thing for my neutrality: You cannot make this girl yours. Not ever. Leave her be, or I will destroy you. *I* am your only daughter, for good or ill."

By now Pitch was less than a dozen feet from Katherine. The snow was blinding. He looked up at her. The look on his face changed from deepest mourning to calculating evil. He seemed on the verge of laughing.

"Yes, my daughter," he said with a sneer. "I will not touch her."

Those were the last words Katherine was to hear for a long, long time.

Chapter Four

Djinnis and Jests

It had been a long day for everyone in Santoff Claussen. Unpacking is always wearying, even when using magic.

Without the robot djinni, however, it would have been exhausting. The djinni had been particularly useful when North had summoned it to unload the train. The djinni's strength was almost unlimited, so it had been able to carry many dozens of large bundles and to give every child in the village a piggyback ride at the same time.

"Thanks, Djinni," called out the youngest William as the metal robot dropped all the Williams and their belongings at their house.

"It was my pleasure," said the djinni in its usual way—crisp and exact and with a chimelike quality, as though it were a talking music box.

North, Ombric, Toothiana, and Bunnymund were busy settling into the comforting hollow of Big Root. The interior of the gigantic tree was tidier than they had left it. While they had been gone, the owls had organized the insects and squirrels into a very efficient cleaning brigade.

North, Ombric, and Bunnymund were scouring the library's newly constituted volumes for any hints that could lead them to Mother Nature's whereabouts, while Toothiana, who also spoke fluent owl, quizzed the wise birds on many points of mutual interest. They were desperate to begin their attempt to rescue Katherine.

From the very beginning, the Guardians had the ability to feel the thoughts and emotions of one another when needed. If one Guardian was in the next room or on the other side of the globe from the others, a call for help could be sensed. But that made it all the more strange that they had heard nothing from Katherine. And they were deeply alarmed that the woman who had taken both Katherine and Pitch was, in fact, Pitch's daughter. Though this Mother Nature clearly possessed enormous power, the Guardians had no clue as to how she had acquired it. They weren't even certain of the extent of her powers. Or whether she was good, evil, or both.

North was particularly frustrated and echoed

all their thoughts. "We know more about making chocolate milk than we do about Pitch's daughter and how she came to be this so-called . . . Nature Mother or Mother Nature. We're supposed to be the wisest men on the—"

Bunnymund felt obliged to interrupt his friend. "The two of you are indeed *men,* and you possess an impressive amount of knowledge for humans of your generations. But, my dear North, must I remind you that I am a Pooka and not a man?"

Sometimes Bunnymund's precise and exact nature could be inadvertently funny . . . or inadvertently irritating. Often at the same time. North looked at the enormous rabbit, who stood even taller than himself. He poked a single finger at one of Bunnymund's impressively large ears. "Holy smoke, you're right! I've never noticed your ears."

Bunnymund blinked twice. One ear twitched slightly. As did his nose. "Really? You never noticed my ears? Oh. I understand," he responded. "That was an example of the peculiar human method of communication known as 'sarcasm.'"

"Or a joke." North smirked. "Someday I'll make you laugh, Bunnymund."

"Me, laugh?" The rabbit looked particularly baffled. "That would be historic. Pookas don't laugh."

North grinned. "No kidding."

"Actually, no. I mean, yes. Well, either way, I'm not, as you say, 'kidding.' Pookas never laugh, as far as I know, and have difficulty in kidding."

"I *know*!" said North.

"Then why did you say it? Oh! You were restating

an obvious fact, to underscore your perception that I needn't have stated the fact in the first place. In other words, you were again being sarcastic and or making a joke."

"Nope," North said. "I was just kidding."

The rabbit's ears, nose, and whiskers were now twitching like mad. "I . . . you . . . that . . . doesn't entirely make sense."

"Really?" asked North. "Are you kidding?"

"No. I mean, yes. Wait. Yes to the first question and no to the second one. But are you kidding or joking with me?"

"Neither," said North. He was deeply pleased. He had finally discovered a way to confound the brilliant rabbit. "I was just being silly."

"Look," said Bunnymund, twitching all over, "I have tried to embrace this thing you call 'humor,' but I do not see the difference between 'kidding' and 'joking' and 'being silly.'"

"Or jesting?" North said.

"That . . . Well . . . it's . . ."

"Or making a quip?"

"No . . . I mean . . ."

"How about a wisecrack?"

"A crack? In something solid? How can that have wisdom?!" asked the rabbit.

"It can't. It just needs to tickle your funny bone," North said, smiling.

The rabbit, however, was panting with frustration. "What are you talking about?! There is no such bone in any known creature. Humor is a mental activity, and it has nothing to do with the skeletal system. To claim so is complete nonsense!"

"EXACTLY!!!" bellowed North.

Ombric had been deliberately ignoring his two comrades. He was buried deep in one of Bunnymund's egg-shaped books.

Ombric was astounded: The rabbit had vast records of all the natural occurrences of the Earth. This wasn't unexpected. He was a creature attuned to nature, more so than any human. But it was how his books were written that was so surprising—in the highly technical phrasing that was typical to Pookan literature. The Earth was usually described as "the planetoidal orb." Earthquakes were referred to as "high-volume terra firma displacement events," and so on.

Midway through the chapter titled "Peculiar Interstellar Phenomena from the Dawn of Time till Last Tuesday," Ombric found something described as an "extraterrestrial solid matter of some interest hurtled through the atmosphere and into a large body of oceanic fluids in the southern Pan-Pacific region in the two millionth equinox cycle." In other words, a meteor or a shooting star had crashed somewhere in the Pacific Ocean, sometime near the end of the Golden Age. Ombric was startled to discover that soon after this event, the weather on Earth changed profoundly. Before, there had been almost no storms of any kind, but since this meteor had arrived, nature had become far more dramatic. Unpredictable. *Is this the beginning of Mother Nature? Has Pitch's daughter come to be here on a shooting star?* wondered Ombric.

At that instant Nightlight flew through one of Big Root's knothole windows. As the Guardian who was most deeply connected to Katherine, Nightlight always knew before any of them if she was in trouble or not. Now the poor boy looked stricken.

A sudden, terrible dread came to them all. They felt certain that Katherine was in grave peril. The owls began to hoot. Toothiana's feathers stood on end.

Chapter Five

Grab a Tear, Save a Story

THE NIGHT WAS OPPRESSIVELY dark. The stars themselves seemed to shrink. Nestled into the upper branches of Big Root was Katherine's tree house. Though it was empty of Katherine, it was not exactly empty. Kailash, now fully grown, sat dejectedly in an impressively large nest, which also served as the tree house's roof. Being full grown meant Kailash was considerably larger than other species of geese. She was quite large even for her own breed. Her wingspan was roughly forty-five feet, and even while sitting in her nest, she was taller than any man.

But her nature was gentle and her emotions still childlike. She was heartbroken over Katherine's disappearance and could barely raise her long neck to respond to the kind attention of the village children who had snuck away from their own beds to comfort her. Petter and his sister, Sascha; the brothers William; and even Fog, who was usually too sleepy for such late-night adventures, were there. They petted Kailash, smoothed her feathers, and tried to convince her to eat. But the giant goose would only make a sad peeping sound.

Petter, who had a fine sense of how to cheer everyone up, suggested that Mr. Qwerty tell one of Katherine's stories.

He opened himself to read one of Katherine's earlier tales, but his voice cracked and faltered. Tears filled his eyes and spread slowly down the handsome leather binding of his book spine.

None of the children had ever seen a book actually cry, which was not surprising, as there had never before been a book that was able to. But the tears that fell from the page to the soft leaves around Kailash's nest surprised them further. Each tear had inside it a letter or a question mark or some other form of punctuation.

It was Sascha who understood the ramifications of this.

"That's Katherine's handwriting!" She gasped. "Please don't cry, Mr. Qwerty. You're crying out Katherine's stories!"

But this caused the poor book to sob even harder. Tears and letters began to spill out at an alarming rate. If this continued, all of Katherine's stories would be drained away.

The children became desperate, and Kailash also began to weep. They reached out to comfort the goose, then turned at the sound of something landing on the far side of the nest. Nightlight was back! He had been with them earlier and had not seemed like himself at all. He was moody, dark, and almost afraid. Then he had left hurriedly. But now he was like the Nightlight of old. He flashed and flickered and grabbed at every fallen tear. Nightlight had amazing abilities with tears. The children had seen this before. He'd once taken their tears and used them to repair his broken diamond dagger that could cut through any armor. But these tears were different. He cradled them in his hands with extraordinary tenderness, as though he held a most delicate treasure. These were Katherine's words and thoughts. This was a treasure that must never be lost. He tucked the wordy tears into his pocket.

Then he looked from the children to Kailash to poor Mr. Qwerty, who thankfully had stopped his sobs. What hope could he offer them? He knew Katherine was in terrifying peril, and he had no idea how to help her. How could he possibly comfort his friends—Katherine's friends?

He felt himself dimming again. Now they'd see for themselves his own desperation.

But Nightlight was a creature of light, and he could shine or feel more in a shadow than any other being. So of course he was the first to see, in the evening shade of Big Root, a light in the sky coming toward them. A sort of lustrous, radiant cloud.

He could feel his hope returning, and he

brightened, leaning toward the light. The others turned to see what he was looking at. One by one, they cried out as they began to see the cloud, a cloud unlike any they'd ever seen—one that left them feeling that hope can sometimes travel in the darkest night.

CHAPTER SIX

The Sandman Cometh

MOMENTS EARLIER NORTH HAD been in mid-sentence when Nightlight had flown suddenly out the window. The boy was frantic to help Katherine, and North had been trying to calm him. For all his bravery and powers, Nightlight was not used to controlling his feelings. Especially feelings like hurt and worry. He wanted to do something. He wanted to help Katherine right then!

North was the closest to understanding what Nightlight was going through, for he had been almost as wild and carefree when he was a lad. Why, he'd lived as a wild child of the Russian forest, raised by Cossack bandits, which is almost the same as being raised by bears. But his attempts to ease Nightlight's anxiousness had lasted about six words before the boy vanished.

Bunnymund sensed North's concern. "In my observations, beings between childhood and adulthood are even more prone to confusing behavior than during any other of the confusing times that inflict most species," the Pooka said.

"He wants to think he can figure everything out for himself," said North, eyeing the rabbit. "A characteristic common in many species, no matter their age." He poked one of Bunnymund's ears.

"I don't know what you're trying to infer, North," said Bunnymund. "I do not *like* to figure everything out. I simply always do!"

Before North could make a snappy response, they became keenly aware of an intense sensation of lightness around them. Not only was there an otherworldly glow to the air inside the tree, but gravity itself seemed to have less pull. They literally felt light on their feet.

"Is someone casting spells?" asked Ombric, glancing around at the others.

A soothing sound enveloped them. Ombric hazarded a guess as to its origin. "It's like the falling sand from a thousand hourglasses."

Under normal circumstances, the orb at the tip of North's sword would have sent out some sort of alarm, but evidently, it found nothing to be alarmed about. Even when the three Guardians began to float from the floor—first a few inches, then higher and higher—the orb stayed silent. Graceful twists of golden glowing sand ebbed up through the floor-boards, pushing them gently but firmly out the giant knothole window and up toward Big Root's upper branches.

As they floated ever higher, none of them, oddly, sensed they were in any danger. Rather, they felt incredibly calm, as though this unprecedented occurrence was simply the way things were somehow supposed to be, which was equally odd. Were they all being drugged? Was this some new magic? If so, they sensed it wasn't a dark sort.

As they approached the treetop, the whorls of sand seemed to be settling more at their feet. To their amazement, they could see that every other creature of Santoff Claussen, human or otherwise, was also floating through the evening sky. Bear, Petrov the horse, even the Spirit of the Forest and Queen Toothiana—they were all rising up and rotating around Big Root.

When they all reached the top and were level with Katherine's tree house, they saw Kailash surrounded by the children. Those in the nest were transfixed by something else. Just above them floated a rotund little man. He had wild swirling golden hair, and he seemed to be glowing from within.

Nightlight stood just below the little man, and as the villagers watched, he began to kneel, as though the man were a king of some kind. The man seemed very friendly; his smile was radiant. It was a smile of total reassurance and gave all who saw it a feeling of intense well-being. Not joy, but something akin to a sleepy peace. A sort of not-a-worry-in-the-world sensation. None of them, not even the Guardians, were able to do anything more than gaze at this gentle fellow. And though he did not speak, they felt as though they heard him say a single whispered phrase: *Time now for a dream*. Then, with a wave of his little hands, the sand began to spin around them. It did not sting, nor did it get in their eyes. It felt rather like the tickling of a soft bed sheet. Then everyone, right down to Bear, fell into a deep, restful sleep.

But this was no ordinary sleep: They began to share an experience that seemed like a dream, for it was dreamlike, but every moment of it was amazing, and somehow, they knew it was absolutely true. They felt they were being given a history in the very best way this friendly little man knew how. And they were certain to remember every detail, for Mr. Qwerty, who was the only one not asleep, was recording the story of this dream experience on his pages. He knew Katherine would not mind. She loved a good story.

This one might also help save her life. And here was how it began. . . .

Chapter Seven

A Dream Pause

My name is Sanderson Mansnoozie, and I have no age.

My story is the story of many dreams. Dreams do not exist within the realm of hours or minutes or any measure of the day. They live in the space between the tick and the tock. Before the tolling of the bell, past the dawn, and beyond the velvet night. I am from a place that was a dream, a place called the Golden Age. And though it may be a place of the past, it is not gone. The dream of it lives still.

My telling it to you will make that so.

I was once a Star Captain in the Golden Age, born to guide the stars that would not stay still. Stars are an amazing phenomenon—all but the rarest stay in place. You see them in the night sky, and you always will. But a few—a precious few—are restless, driven on and on by too much energy or curiosity or even anger. . . . These are the ones we call "shooting stars."

As a star pilot, I belonged to the League of Star Captains, a cheerful brotherhood devoted to the granting of wishes. We each had a wandering star that we commanded. In the tip of our star was our cabin, a bright compact place, much like an opulent bunk bed. We journeyed wherever we pleased, passing planets at random and listening to the wishes that were made to us as we passed. If a wish was worthy, we were honor-bound to answer it. We would send a dream to whomever had made

the wish. The dream would go to that person as they slept, and within this dream, there would be a story.

If the story was powerful enough, the person would remember it forever, and it would help guide them in their quest to make the wish come true. These dreams were considered one of the greatest treasures of the Golden Age. But to create the dream in the first place, we had to be asleep. So we were often asleep and dreaming, even as we flew, and our stars would awaken us if trouble lurked.

And trouble wasn't difficult to find. Dream Pirates prowled every galaxy. They were nasty, stunted creatures who lived by stealing dreams. At first they ruthlessly plundered these dream treasures of the Golden Age for the bounty they could raise for their return. But then they discovered an even more wicked motive for this crime. If they consumed a dream, it made them stronger, tougher, and more powerful in every evil way.

So we Star Captains fought hundreds of battles with the Dream Pirates, at least until the great war that ended them. We weren't without help—the other planets and Constellations of the Golden Age banded together and formed the greatest fleet in the known universe, led by the most brilliant and fearless captain in history, Kozmotis Pitchiner, Lord High General of the Galaxies. It was Lord Pitch (as he was called by his sailors) who sailed unceasingly to every corner of the heavens and hunted down legion after legion of Dream Pirates. Though he was victorious and had become the greatest hero of the Golden Age, he paid a most terrible price. And that is where this story of my life takes an unexpected turn.

The tragedy of Pitch and what brought him low

became the center of my journey. It is the story of Pitch and his lost daughter.

Of how she became lost.

Of how Pitch was broken past healing.

And of how his daughter became the one you call "Mother Nature."

CHAPTER EIGHT

The Heart Becomes the Hunted

The War of the Dream Pirates was vicious and bloody. The pirates knew that if they lost, they would never again be as powerful as they were at that very moment. So they became more clever, devious, and cruel with their tactics: They would destroy whole planets. Extinguish stars. Eliminate entire Constellations.

For eons the pirates had been seen as dangerous criminals. Now the people of the Golden Age viewed them as an evil that had to be eradicated. Soon hate became the center of how this war was waged, and hate is a powerful force.

It can make bad men worse and good men nearly mad.

Lord Pitch had been noble and fair at the start of his campaign. He'd fought honorably against the pirates. When he bested their ships, he took the survivors prisoner. He fed them well and urged them to renounce their wretched ways.

But the pirates saw this thread of humanity as a weakness, a weakness that could be used against Lord Pitch. They'd thus far failed in their attempts to assassinate him, and their attempts had been many. Now, however, they realized with cold calculation, if they failed to kill him in body, they would simply destroy his spirit.

They began to hunt for that which mattered most to the valiant sailor: his family. Lord Pitch kept his wife and child housed safely on the small moon of a planet deep in the heart of the

Constellation Orion. It was a lovely moon and was well protected by the many asteroids that encircled it. Each asteroid was a small fortress, armed with a platoon of the elite of the Golden Age Armies.

Lord and Lady Pitchiner were doting parents, their palace a thrilling place to raise their young daughter, Emily Jane. She was a wild and joyful child, with raven-black hair as thick and flowing as a horse's mane, which was fitting, as she was always on the run. Like her father, she loved to sail. She was constantly in her own small schooner, venturing around her moon and its asteroids.

Lady Pitchiner, ever vigilant in her care of their only child, often ordered Emily Jane to stay close, to take a guard with her, or simply to stay home. But Emily Jane disobeyed her mother frequently. She couldn't stop herself from slipping out alone and doing as she pleased. Her father loved his girl's wild heart, so he turned a blind eye to her disobedient sailing ways.

Fate can be as peculiar as any dream or story, for it was one of these little secret adventures that saved Emily Jane's life.

Dream Pirates had been reported off the tip of Orion's sword. Lord Pitch hurriedly said his farewells to his wife and daughter before preparing to hunt down the scoundrels. The family never liked saying good-bye; they tried not to think of the dangers that would be faced. But this time Emily Jane had made for her father a silver locket containing her picture. He was very pleased by it and put it around his neck as he kissed her.

"I'll be back soon," he told her.

"Promise?" she said.

"On my soul," he replied.

Lord Pitch was a man of his word. And he reassured himself that his family was safe. Their moon home had many defenses against a large attack.

But the Dream Pirates had not planned a large attack. They had something more intimately sinister in mind.

Several dozen pirates, shadowy and expert, slipped past every guard, every outpost, every defense and made their way to Lord Pitch's villa.

The villa was spacious, columned, almost castlelike. It was carved from moonstone, so the rooms had a soothing, cool glow of reflected light, even in the darkest night. But this night seemed particularly dark.

All in the villa were asleep except one—Emily Jane. After bedtime she had slipped out her bedroom window and into her schooner docked close by. She hadn't yet traveled far when she spied a school of Star Fish, swimming low in the moon's atmosphere. She loved Star Fish—a favorite game was to tie her schooner to the leader and ride along with them as they swooped and dove through the canyons near her home.

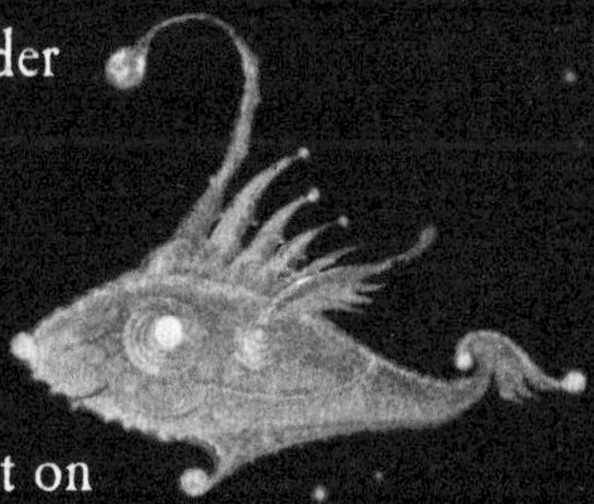

The Dream Pirates, so intent on infiltrating the villa, had not seen the girl sneaking out. Emily Jane had already cast off when the pirates were surrounding the villa and readying to strike. They could feel the sleeping dreams of Lady Pitchiner and of the entire household. To the Dream Pirates, dreams were like blood to a vampire. Dreams made them hungry and sometimes stupid. Could they feel the dreams of Lord Pitch's daughter? They were too impatient and crazed to make sure. "She must be in there somewhere," they reasoned.

And so they charged.

A Dream Pirate attack is swift and ragged. Like awkward phantoms, the pirates often fly in lurches and jerks, and they usually destroy everything that gets in their way.

Lady Pitchiner startled awake as the pirates smashed their way through the house, coming closer and closer to where she lay. She could hear the alarms sounding, but would help come in time? She doubted it. She ran into Emily Jane's bedroom and locked the door. But the bed was empty. The covers hadn't even been pulled down.

Good! Lady Pitchiner thought. *She's out on her ship!* For once, she was thankful rather than angry that her daughter was so rebellious.

The pirates were smashing down the door.

Lady Pitchiner had only an instant to act. *They'll be looking for us both,* she thought. So she grabbed a large doll and held it in her arms, as if it were Emily Jane, and sat very still. The door splintered into pieces, and the pirates poured in. Lady Pitchiner knew the awful fate of those taken by Dream Pirates—their souls sucked dry of dreams, leaving them to become mindless slaves . . . or worse.

They must be made to think that we have died, she thought desperately as the pirates clamored closer. Keeping just enough of the doll exposed under her cape so the pirates would see it, she ran for the window. Straight into and through it. The glass shattered. Lady Pitchiner was gone.

The pirates pressed at the window, staring down. The fall was more than a mile.

Emily Jane had heard the alarms and the explosions echoing through the canyons she was coasting. She knew the ruckus could only be coming from her home. She knew the sound of a Dream Pirate attack. They had attacked her father's ship when she and her mother had first come this moon. And though she was wild, she was not foolish. She stayed with the Star Fish. Perhaps if she rode among them, she would not be seen. The Star Fish swam swiftly through the canyons, in a near panic from the sounds of battle.

Between gaps in the canyons peaks, Emily Jane watched in horror as her palace was riddled with explosions. She could make out the window of her own room, then the awful sound of shattering glass, and there was the unmistakable figure of her mother falling.

Emily Jane turned away. She closed her eyes tightly and would not open them; she let the Star Fish take her where they would. The Star Fish darted on and on, away from the embattled moon, through the rings of meteors, and out into the ocean of space. Soon Emily Jane could no longer hear anything but the lulling sound of the wind as she was pulled farther and farther from her doomed home and into the eternity of space.

CHAPTER NINE

A Little Girl Lost and a Titan Found

And so Emily Jane traveled far from her home and far from her sorrow, until she came to an unexpectedly safe place—the Constellation called Typhan. Before the War of the Dream Pirates, Typhan had been a maker of storms and was a powerful ally of the Golden Age. He could conjure up solar winds so vast and terrible, they would scatter whole fleets of Dream Pirate galleons when required.

But the wily Dream Pirates had managed to ravage him and render him harmless: They had extinguished the stars that had been his eyes. Once blinded, he could no longer see the pirates as they attacked. And they had been merciless, killing so many of his stars that his once-vivid outline was nearly gone. He was now a forgotten ghost of his former self, and he had lost the will to make storms or to fight. He was a mournful, pitiful Titan. Only the harmless Star Fish ever swam among Typhan's few remaining stars and moons.

Now, as the Star Fish weaved their way past Typhan's head, Emily Jane was as blind to the damaged giant as he was to her. Her thoughts were only of her poor mother, her vanished home, and the feeling of being as lost as any child could be. "Father," she cried at last. "Come find me! Please! Please!! I am so alone!"

Typhan heard these cries. He had only heard the taunts and laughter of the Dream Pirates since his sight was destroyed. He thought he would never again hear a voice that was not forged by cruelty.

"Child?" he whispered. "How come you here?"

Even in a whisper, his voice could fill a galaxy, but his was a strong, unthreatening voice, like a summer storm that has recently passed.

Startled, Emily Jane looked up and saw what remained of the starlight giant. Like all Golden Age children, she had been schooled in the names and shapes of the Constellations, so she immediately recognized his dimmed face.

Through tears, she told Typhan who she was and all the awfulness of her journey. This stirred Typhan, and for the first time since his blinding, he felt an echo of his former might. They had both been victims of the Dream Pirates and had been left to lonely fates. He summoned up a breeze that took Emily Jane and her Star Fish to a moon near the stars of his right ear. The travellers were exhausted, and resting was very welcome. As they landed among the powdery craters, Typhan spoke once more.

"Child," he said. "You are not alone."

Those words were like a shield of comfort for Emily Jane. She felt safer, and even hopeful. And as she fell into a long, weary sleep, she thought over and over: *Somehow, my father will find me.*

Chapter Ten

The Dream Becomes a Nightmare

When word reached Lord Pitch that his home and family were under attack, he knew he had been duped. There were no pirates waiting where he had been told. So he pushed his fleet to return with a speed none thought possible. The palace, and most of his moon, was now nothing but scorched ruins. The pirates were reboarding their sleek escape vessels when Lord Pitch's warships surrounded them. They never expected him to return so swiftly.

Lord Pitch wanted these pirates alive. "My wife and child may be among them," he told his lieutenants.

The pirates were impossibly outgunned. They knew it was hopeless to fight, and they also knew they could count on Lord Pitch's compassion. They surrendered without the firing of a single shot.

But as they were hauled aboard Lord Pitch's flagship, they did not face the same noble warrior they had come to begrudgingly respect. They faced a man on the brink of madness.

"My wife and daughter? Where are they?" Lord Pitch demanded.

The captain of the Dream Pirates said with a sneer, "We were denied the pleasure of draining them of their dreams."

"Because you were caught?"

"No, my lord."

"Have you harmed them?"

"No, my lord," replied the captain. Its lips curled into a small, satisfied smile. "They are dead."

Lord Pitch stood stoically. He was a gentleman of the Golden Age, a commander of its armies. Even now, he felt he must maintain his judgment and composure. But the pirate captain was too keen to bring forth his hurts.

"Your lady so feared our company that she threw herself to her doom, and the child with her," the captain gloated.

Lord Pitch could barely speak. He looked from one pirate to another. "Is this true?"

The captain grinned. "'Tis true, my lord. I saw it myself. As did we all."

Lord Pitch, bringing his face within inches of the captain's, said with a measured calm, "Then feast your eyes on mine. They are the last things you will ever see." And with startling suddenness, he drew his sword and cut the captain's head from its body.

He stepped quickly to the next pirate, and before another word could be said, he sliced again. Another head tumbled to the deck. The pirates gasped and pulled against their chains, but Lord Pitch continued on.

His own crew shuffled and murmured uneasily. Was this their general? The most gallant of the Golden Age? Lord Pitch was methodical and never paused. All the pirates, and Lord Pitch's mercy, were dead in less time than it takes to sing a song.

CHAPTER ELEVEN

A Stormy Relationship

Emily Jane's life with Typhan suited her nature. He had been a god of storms, and now he delighted in conjuring up tempests for her to ride. At first she rode her Star Fish over the waves of solar wind that Typhan blew, but in time he taught her the trick of making storms herself. He anointed her as his daughter, and from then on, she could wield the power of the heavens. Wind, starlight, gravity were hers to command. She now was a sister of the heavens and was honor-bound to use her power only for good.

Emily Jane never tired of summoning playful

squalls; she rode them until she was exhausted. It was the only peace she knew from the heartaches that ate away at her. Where was her father? Why did he not come to find her? Typhan was kind; he even loved her. In time she regarded him with awe, but awe is not affection or love. It didn't heal her pain. She stayed with Typhan because she hoped against hope that if she remained in one place, there was a chance her father could still find her. But while the Star Fish swam as far as they dared to try to send word of Emily Jane, they could never make it far enough. Days turned into weeks, weeks into months, months into years.

Occasionally, passing wrecks of abandoned ships drifted by the Constellation. Emily Jane became an expert forager. She discovered that the contents inside these ghostly vessels could supply her with all her needs. She positioned dozens of scavenged telescopes all over her small moon so she could be the eyes of Typhan. Food, supplies, clothes, furniture, books—everything she might need—all were found in the abandoned wrecks that strayed close enough to her moon that she or the Star Fish could retrieve them. The hull of a crashed galleon served as her home. So she lived in a sort of ramshackle magnificence. There was even treasure. Great heaping chests of it, which she stored in the moon's small, hollow core. But the more treasure she amassed, the less the treasure came to mean to her. She even began to hate it. It reminded her of the past. Of her home. Of the Golden Age.

In those early weeks and months with Typhan, she had scanned the heavens in every direction, each hour on the hour, ever hopeful, looking for her father's flagship. But the years bore on without a single sighting. *He has forgotten me,* she decided one fateful day. It was the morning of her sixteenth birthday.

She had tried to forget the date. Year after year, her only wish had been a simple one: that her father would come. But ten birthdays had passed, and each one left her harder and more bitter.

On this day a ship finally appeared in the distance! Her hope came back. She could tell in an instant that it wasn't a Dream Pirate vessel. Their ships were always twisted, spiked, and foul to look at. This was a Golden Age craft to be sure. Elegant of line and sail. It was beautiful . . . too beautiful. It was no warship. But it did not fly the flag of her father. It was a peaceful liner and nothing more.

Why has Father never come? she wondered bitterly. And she felt an anger that clouded her good sense. She hated her father now. She hated the world that she had so ached to return to. She'd rather stay lost. And in that dreadful moment, something changed in her. Her heart became consumed with rage.

Typhan could feel that something was terribly wrong.

"Daughter?" he whispered. "What do you see? Friend or foe?"

Her answer surprised even herself. "I see only foes!" And without warning, she raised up a murderous storm.

Typhan knew the sound of pain and rage. He feared that she had lost her reason.

"Daughter!" he cried out. "What ship approaches?"

"Not the ship I hope for!" she shouted back. Her violent winds sped toward the helpless vessel.

"Stop this tempest!" Typhan ordered her. "We never harm without cause!"

"From now on, my cause is harm!" she screamed.

Typhan knew then that she had gone mad, and gathering all his strength, he sent forth winds to counter hers.

But her rage was equal to Typhan's goodness, and she fought him, hurling a galaxy of hate-filled torrents at the ancient colossus.

"Daughter! Stop!" he pleaded, summoning every last ounce of strength he possessed.

"You are not my father!" Emily Jane shrieked.

Meteors! Comets! Hunks of broken planets came smashing into Typhan's stars and shattered the Golden Age galleon that neared.

The old Constellation's heart was cleaved by her words. He was stunned and heartsick. Her deeds were a betrayal that could not be forgiven.

"From forever on, you are cursed!" he bellowed, stunned and heartsick. "You have broken your vow!"

It scorched his soul to punish her so harshly, to cast her out of his life. But an oath had been broken. So with one mighty blast of his lungs, he sent Emily Jane's moon shooting away from him. It flew at such a speed that it began to brighten, brighten till a hot white light burned, until the moon itself became a shooting star streaking through space like a spear.

Emily Jane fled to the moon's hollow core just as the old galleon where she had slept was burned to ash. Her telescopes disintegrated. In nanoseconds everything on her moon's surface was gone. Because she had fled to the moon's core, she became entombed by the melting chest of treasure for which she cared nothing. Emily Jane was indeed doomed.

She would have to live within this new star's center and never leave it until it crashed.

If only she had known her father thought her dead.

If only she and her father had known the truth.

Two hearts that had once been united at the center of the Golden Age would not have become hardened, embittered, and so very cruel. These wounded hearts would not have brought an end to the Age of Wonders.

CHAPTER TWELVE

Stars Cross

This dream continued for all in Santoff Claussen, but the Guardians were taking particular note. They knew, even in this dream state, that they were learning a great deal about Pitch, which could be useful in fighting him. But they also began to feel the pity Katherine had felt. Pitch had not always been evil. His heart was once as strong and good as theirs. But for Nightlight, this was a feeling that confused him. He thought only in simple terms. He didn't want to feel pity. He wanted only to save Katherine, and he could not see how pity could help him.

Then Sanderson Mansnoozie appeared and

became part of the story he had been telling. The dream had been so intense and dramatic that even in their deep sleep, the villagers and Guardians were glad to at last see him. Sandy had a manner both soothing and blissful. He smiled, sending a blanket of calm to one and all, and then continued the tale. . . .

We in the League of Star Captains quickly became aware of this "new" star. I was born into a family of Star Captains. For generations we had steered stars to every corner of the universe, our primary duty to bestow the wishes made to our stars. But the stars we harnessed needed greater and greater speed, for the Dream Pirates were especially intent on capturing Wishing Stars. You see, in all the galaxies, there are few things with more dreams in them than a Wishing Star. These stars are concentrated dream matter, and their pilots are the key to unlocking those dreams. When someone made a wish that was judged worthy, then a Star Captain would send back one of those dreams to help that person fulfill their wish.

But within each star was stored tens of thousands of undreamed dreams that were made by our brethren since time began.

And so when I heard of this wild new shooting star, I pursued it. I didn't know its origins. I didn't know Emily Jane was at its cursed core. But I saw that this star could outpace any Dream Pirate vessel. If I was to saddle it, I would need to be clever.

Many other Star Captains were also after this star, but it had outrun them all. Shooting stars are generally very solitary. They live for speed and wildness. But I had noticed that this particular star would sometimes slow down for schools of Star

Fish. The Star Fish seemed to have a kinship with the star, which was most intriguing.

My brother Star Captains tried to sneak up on the slowing star when it neared a school of Star Fish, but they failed. The star was no fool. It could sense a trap and would blast away, leaving any who chased it choking on its stardust.

I don't like to boast, but I was well liked among the creatures of the cosmos. Star horses and Star Fish have always been my friends. I have a soft spot for them and liked to feed them a star spice they find most delicious, much as you humans do with sugar for your horses. So one day I rode near a school of Star Fish. They were glad to see me and let me swim along. I'd brought supplies of that special spice, and soon they had completely surrounded me, each hovering beside me to have a taste, hiding me completely.

In time the wild star came near.

I waited till it was gliding right by me, keeping pace with us. Then I charged through the Star Fish and lassoed the star with my line. The stun of surprise lasted only a second. The star shot away with more speed than any I'd ever seen, but I held on.

This is not uncommon in trying to catch a wild star. There is an ancient method for bringing them to heel, and I followed it to the letter. I skied along in its fiery wake for ten thousand leagues, pulling myself closer and closer to its burning apex. But it dove and snaked with such fury! It even tried to scrape against a planet or two to knock me off! It seemed . . . enraged, something I'd never witnessed before in a star. It needed to serve my more gentle purposes if only to calm itself—otherwise, it would burn out.

It was the toughest fight I've ever had with a star. Days are difficult to measure in deep space, but it took me the equal of fourteen Earth days to finally tame this wild one. And in the end it was tame in only one regard: It would let me steer it.

Not a lot is known about shooting stars. Mortals, of course, never have a chance to do more than watch and wish when they see one. But something happens when you master a star. You come to understand it. Each has an individual personality that you can sense and feel. All are vivid, but this star had an energy that far exceeded any I'd known. It had a voice. It spoke to me. At first it would not tell me its name or anything about its past, but in time it came to trust me. It could tell I meant it no harm, that I wanted to be its friend and ally. And a friend is like a savior to one so angry and lost. But still the star did not tell me its name.

We sailed from one end of the cosmos to the other. I would answer dreams whispered up to us. When the Dream Pirates would attack us, my star would not pause, as most stars did, but would charge them head-on, fearlessly.

Together we won every battle.

Then for a year we traveled in peace. Not once did we happen upon a single pirate. We were curious about our good fortune. In the vast reaches of space, news is slow to arrive. Then word came that the war with the pirates was over. It was said Lord Pitch had been victorious and all the Dream Pirates imprisoned. The Golden Age was safe again! And I thought this would be a cause for great celebration for my star and me. But upon hearing this news, my star broke free of my will. It flew at breakneck speed, trying to crash into any heavenly body in its path—planets, stars, fields of asteroids. I could barely keep it from destroying us both.

Then, when it began to careen directly toward a small green planet, a thousand wishes rose up from the children of that doomed world. These weren't the common hopeful wishes sent to a shooting star. These were terror-filled wishes. "Please, bright star, don't kill us."

I urged my star to stop. *Think! Think of the children who fear your coming! You are no better than a Dream Pirate!*

And at that moment my star stopped.

If shooting stars ever stop, they quickly become a sun. It takes only a few minutes for this process to become irreversible. In all my eons as a Star Master, I had never ridden a star that had just . . . stopped. I sat at my controls and wondered what my wild star would do next. Then

I heard what sounded like crying from the star's core, and the words, "My name . . . is Emily Jane. Please, I do not want to be feared."

Chapter Thirteen

Who Does a Star Wish Upon?

I listened to the long, sad tale of Emily Jane. Now I understood her mysteries. She was driven by a child's rage that had never been soothed, never been healed, and now this rage had the power to destroy worlds. She was moments away from becoming a stationary star. If she continued to refuse to move, she would never fly again. Her anger or strength wouldn't ever again threaten any living being. This would be the safest outcome, surely, but what would it do to Emily Jane? To be imprisoned forever in her star with nothing but her anger did not seem . . . fair. Terrible events had twisted her better instincts. But if she could tame her fury . . .

So I offered her a choice.

Emily Jane! You can stay here with your rage until you burn yourself out. Or . . . fly again. Let me guide you, and together we will do wonders.

There was only silence from her. I added hopefully, *Perhaps we can find your father and with him . . . peace.*

The minutes went by and still Emily Jane said nothing. There were mere seconds left before she'd become fixed forever in this spot. In that moment she suddenly flamed brightly and jerked forward just a little.

"I will ride," she whispered with a new calm. And before I could communicate how pleased I was, she shot away with a speed that took my breath.

From the start, she had been difficult to steer, always pulling against me, so now I feared the worst. But after that initial burst of speed, she followed my lead contentedly. We inquired about the whereabouts of her father from any ship or planet we neared, but in these faraway regions of the galaxies, very little was known. So we worked our way toward the great center of the Golden Age, to the Constellation of Zeus. It was a peaceful journey. And when wishes came, Emily Jane listened.

She heard every kind of wish there was. Wishes for ponies and pets. Wishes for riches. Wishes for revenge on enemies. Wishes for love. Emily Jane came to understand all the things that people yearn for. In time she could see the difference between wishes that were worthy of being granted and those that were not.

"People are often . . . confused," she said to

me one quiet night as we streaked through the sky. "They want what they don't need, or can't use, or won't ever make them whole."

True. I was proud that she was learning.

"I think all wishes are the same, really," she continued. "Whether they ask for this, that, or the other, what they are really asking for is happiness."

And what do you wish? I wondered. *What would make you happy?*

She did not answer for a while.

The silence of a peaceful night in the deep oceans of space can feel almost holy. The vast darkness is dotted with stars that go on and on—farther than any light or thought can seem to travel. But they do. In that quiet solitude that wrapped around us, Emily Jane answered my question.

"I wish to be washed clean of my old life. To

let go of my tide of sorrows and find my way to a new shore."

This was a good and worthy wish. It was a wish I wanted to grant.

But fate had other plans.

Chapter Fourteen

Hope Becomes a Weapon Most Foul

We were leagues away from any planet, and no other wishes could reach us. And I began to think about Emily Jane's wish. To answer her wish would take all my thought and wisdom. I must go into a sleepier trance to fashion an Answer Dream.

It is during this trance that a Star Captain must let the star steer itself and be on the lookout for any trouble. Our travels had been peaceful for so long that I had no worries, and Emily Jane had always been up to the task of dealing with any attack.

But there was a danger neither of us had foreseen.

In all the time that Emily Jane had been trapped in her star, she had been dreaming one dream over and over: that her father would rescue her.

Lord Pitch had decided that imprisoning the pirates was a worse fate than death, so the Dream Pirates were confined to a planet-size prison on the other side of the cosmos. But they could still detect a dream no matter how far away and faint it might be.

They had heard Emily Jane's dream.

At first it had puzzled them. How could this be? *The child of Pitch died in a raid years before,* they thought. But every night they heard the dream again and again, and after a time they realized the dream was indeed coming from Lord Pitch's daughter. So they hatched an awful plan.

The Dream Pirates knew how badly the loss of his family had wounded Lord Pitch. And he was their one and only jailer. He guarded the single door into the prison that held them; it was such a grim and dark place. Made from giant plates of dark matter, it was a place where no being from outside could ever hear or feel any pirate who coiled inside. Only Lord Pitch could hear them faintly. He had volunteered to be their single guard. He felt he had nothing left since the loss of his family.

The Dream Pirates, with the help of the other dark creatures imprisoned with them, listened each night to Emily Jane's faint dream until they knew the sound of her voice and could imitate it. Then, one awful night, they huddled next to the single door and whispered to Lord Pitch, in his daughter's voice, the one thing they hoped would set them free. "Please, Daddy. Please, please, please open the door."

Emily Jane? he thought to her. He pulled the silver locket from his tunic pocket and stared at the photograph inside. He did not stop to wonder how she could possibly be inside the prison.

"Daddy, I'm trapped in here with these shadows, and I'm scared. Please open the door. Help me, Daddy, please."

What father could ignore such a plea? Lord Pitch opened the door, his aching heart suddenly hopeful that Emily Jane was somehow alive and near enough to be saved.

He opened the door and sealed his doom.

The Dream Pirates poured out and enveloped him. The cold, calculated betrayal was more than any being could withstand. The locket fell from Lord Pitch's neck. With his hope shattered, his heart withered and he died inside. At first he resisted valiantly, but there was no fight left in him. Numb and utterly empty, he let the dark creatures take his soul. And they did—they possessed him completely.

He became their leader, their king, their warlord.

With Lord Pitch as their general, the Golden Age had lost its greatest strength, its greatest ally. And so began the awful second War of the Dream Pirates, and Pitch was proving unstoppable.

But now he could hear Emily Jane's dream. He had ten times the wicked thirst and need for dreams as his pirates. And her dream haunted him and fed his new hunger.

All this had happened without our knowing. Emily Jane's newfound hope was like a beacon, drawing evil and awfulness toward us.

Chapter Fifteen

The Most Bitter Reckoning

The first harpoon that hit us came as a surprise, but by the second and third, I was fully awake and Emily Jane was already charging the Dream Pirate galleon that had fired upon us. It was a massive vessel—tarnished, ragged, and beastly to behold.

Its decks were swarming with Dream Pirates, who fired harpoon after harpoon with withering swiftness. But Emily Jane displayed amazing agility at dodging their rusted dagger points and using her blazing tail to burn us free of the first harpoons that hit.

She was heading straight for the ship's bow,

her star fires flaming with determination. I braced for our impact, but the pirate galleon swerved to port at the last instant. We shaved so close to the ship, we could see the shadowy faces of the grisly crew who leered and taunted us as we passed. At the ship's helm stood its captain, tall, gaunt, and unmistakable. It was Lord Pitch himself. Or at least what he had become.

His skin was now a spectral white, his eyes dark and soulless; he was a creature to be feared.

For Emily Jane, this was a shock beyond all reckoning. Her father had arrived at last, but now he was a nightmare come to life.

Then Pitch shouted out to me. "Ahoy, Dream Master!"

I tried to slow Emily Jane, so I could better hear Pitch's hail, and though she pulled against me, she yielded to my maneuver.

"Why do you send this dream of my dead daughter to plague me?" Pitch shouted again.

Before I could send him an answer, Emily Jane implored, her voice trembling with terror, "Please, be careful what you say, Captain Sandy. He is so changed. We can't know what to expect."

I sent this thought, taking care with my words: *The dream this vessel sends you, it is no plague! It is a dream of hope!!*

"I have no hopes!" he bellowed. His voice was edged with rage. "This dream you sent is what killed my soul and made me what I now am! DEATH, I say, to who made me thus!"

Emily Jane had never backed down from a fight. But she understood the madness of rage. Her rage at this man had driven her to the brink of despair. But she had pulled back. Could he? He had not seen her since she was a little girl. If she were free from her star, would he recognize her? Would his hate die as hers had? In an instant her instincts told her a grim truth.

"We must run, Captain Sandy," she said. "I can feel it. If he finds me, we both shall die."

Go then, I agreed. *As fast as you ever have.*

Away we flew. But Pitch's harpoon men were too skilled and quick. Before we could get out of range, a dozen of their weapons slammed into us, their chains linking us to Pitch's galleon. Emily Jane frantically tried to burn them away, but as one disintegrated, three more ensnared us. Our speed no longer mattered, for now we pulled the galleon with us. The pirates winched the chains and inched their malevolent ship closer and closer.

I had fought the Dream Pirates time and again and had never been defeated, but never before had they been led by Pitch. I'd never encountered such fury. But Emily Jane swerved and breached with a power that even Pitch's galleon could not contain. With one great last buck, she snapped free of the chains and we tumbled away.

We spun and spiraled
at speeds beyond

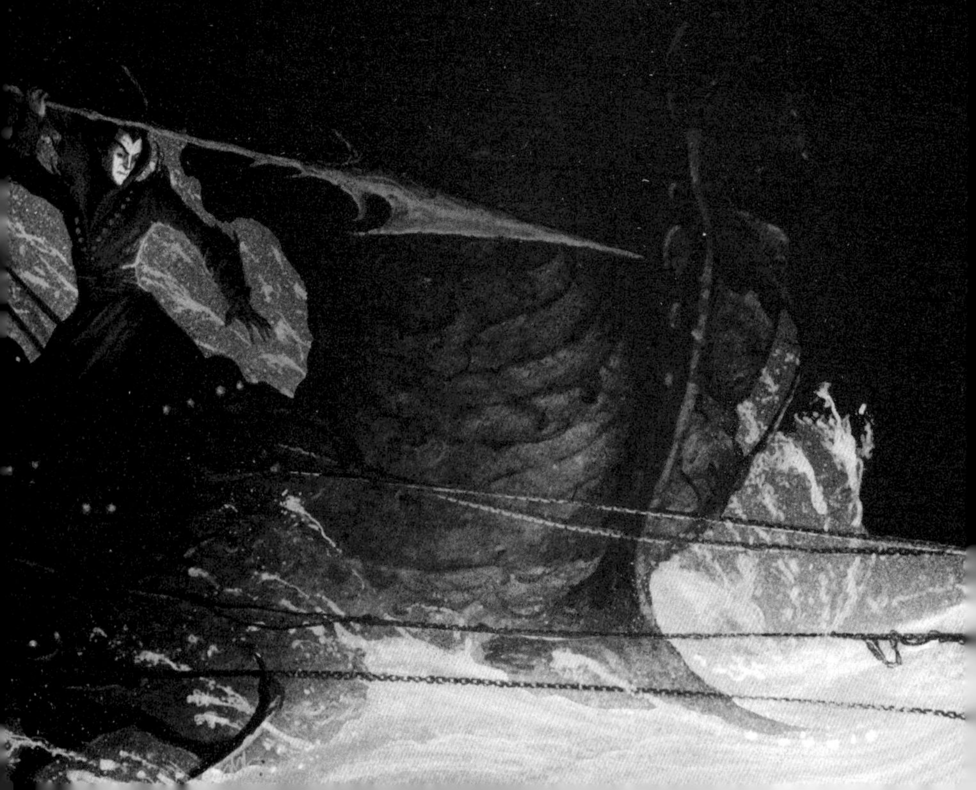

endurance. I remember seeing a small green and blue planet just ahead of us. I could barely stay conscious. I knew we would crash. I could hear the wishes of children coming from the planet, so I pulled at my controls. We must crash over water so as not to harm any child. I could no longer feel or sense Emily Jane. As we plummeted toward a vast ocean, I did hear one thing: a single wish above all the others. It was bright and clear.

"I wish you well" was all

Fig. 1. The star falls.

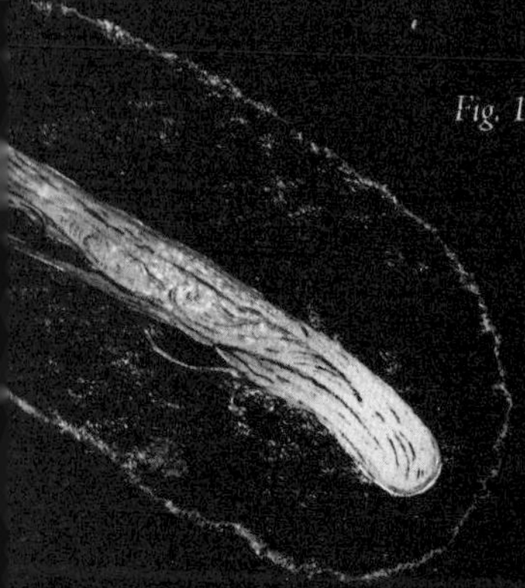

it said, and as I fell unconscious, certain that my star and I were doomed, I thought of that wish and nothing else.

Fig. 2. The star hits the ocean.

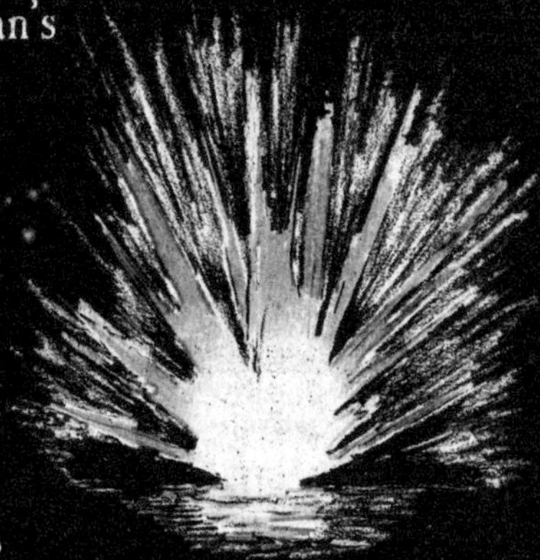

We skipped across the ocean's surface like a giant stone, then came to a spray of water, and all went black for me.

I did not wake for many, many years. When I did, I found that my star was shattered, pulverized into a sandy island. I was awakened by that same voice that had comforted me all those years ago, the voice that had wished me well. It turned out to be your Man in the Moon.

And so it is I come to you, with the Moon's instructions. I will help

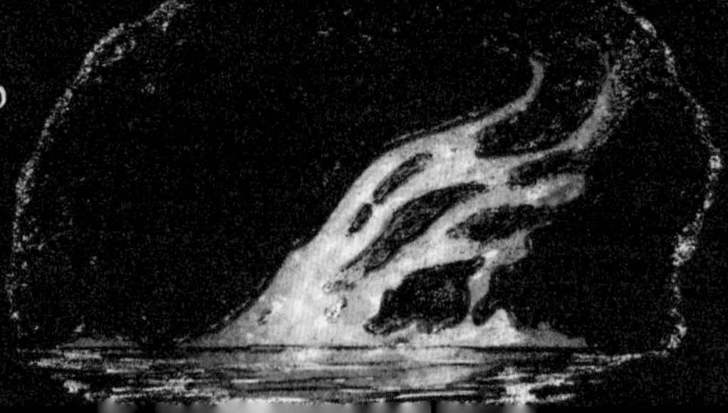

Fig. 3. The smoke clears.

you save your friend, Katherine, and fight Pitch. But to do so, I must finally see the girl who lived in my star, Emily Jane, daughter of Lord Pitch and the one you call Mother Nature.

Fig. 4. The star is now the Island of the Sleepy Sands.

CHAPTER SIXTEEN

Oh, What a Mysterious Morning!

AND AS SANDY REACHED the end of his story, everyone awoke from the dream. They blinked their eyes and roused, surprised to find that it was morning. Those who had fallen asleep while floating in the air around Big Root awoke in their usual beds and under the covers. North was in his customary Cossack bed shirt and sleeping cap. His trusty elfin men were on the floor in a row at the foot of his bed. They snorted awake like a litter of young piglets. Bunnymund was all comfy in his egg-shaped bed, which he always traveled with, his head propped up by half a dozen egg-shaped pillows. He was wearing satin pajamas with matching ear warmers that had small egg-shaped pom-poms dangling from the tips. Bunnymund lifted the egg-shaped patches that covered his eyes and gave his ears a wake-up shake.

Ombric was, of course, roosting in his huge globe, surrounded by his owls. They woke in unison, as always, though Ombric did not hoot as he usually did. Toothiana found herself perched in a marvelous twig structure that hung like a bell from one of the limbs that formed the top of Big Root's canopy. It was the perch she had back in Punjam Hy Loo. *How has it arrived in Santoff Claussen?* she wondered.

The children were in the same place they had started the evening, at the top of Big Root, nestled next to Kailash in her gigantic nest. They looked around, utterly perplexed. The Dream had seemed so real. Yet here they were, feeling rested and ready, but for what, exactly? The host of their dream was nowhere to be seen. Nightlight stood up and looked at the spot where Sandman had hovered. There was nothing. Not even a grain of sand.

Mr. Qwerty peered at his pages. They were filled—the entire dream had been written down, and at the very end was a tiny drawing of Sandman.

Nightlight gazed at the illustrated page. He was unsure what to think about what he saw. But he reached out and touched the sparkling sketch. The drawing was made from a sort of sticky sand. It had been left by Sandman himself!

Golden grains clung to Nightlight's fingertips. He looked at them closely. He could feel the magic in them. Then he had a sort of flash of memory, of a song from so long ago: *Nightlight, bright light, sweet dreams I bestow. . . .*

"Is there a message there, Nightlight?" Petter asked.

Nightlight closed his eyes and held his sand-covered fingertips to his forehead. The sand told him many, many things.

Nightlight rarely, if ever, spoke—only the direst of circumstances could compel him to use his mesmerizing, otherworldly voice. So it was all the more alarming when he quietly replied: "Only that he's gone to help Katherine. And that none of us should follow."

Chapter Seventeen

Nightlight Dawns

THE FIVE GUARDIANS WERE in a full frenzy for the rest of the day. Or more accurately, Ombric, North, Bunnymund, and Toothiana debated all morning while Nightlight remained still and quiet. He watched his friends study grain after grain of Mansnoozie's sand under a never-ending array of magnifying glasses, microscopes, spyglasses, cosmic ray detectors, and even a crystal-clear egg that Bunnymund assured them could pinpoint the precise origin of the sand and its exact age. It did neither.

After hours of testing and studying, the only

conclusion they came to was that this sand was . . . well . . . sand. It obviously had magical properties, but what exactly were those properties, and how were they triggered?

No one knew. And so they argued on, about everything. Whether to try to follow Sandman. How to follow him if they ever could agree to follow him. Where he might have gone and what to do if they found him. Should they split up and try to find Katherine? Should they call the Lunar Lamas? Should they try to contact the Man in the Moon?

And, most irritatingly, why hadn't Sandman asked them to join him? They studied charts, they consulted clouds, they looked into the past, they tried to see the future, they grumbled and worried and fussed.

Though Nightlight remained silent, it was not

without purpose. He had not yet told his friends that he could "read" the sand. Which was not unusual. He spoke only if he thought it necessary. He was always curious about the ways of the "Tall Ones," as he called adults. He did not think of them as smart or intelligent. He thought of them in terms of other qualities, those things that made a Tall One "good": kindness, bravery, trust, fun. But if they were cruel, lied maliciously, or were mean? Then Nightlight viewed them as "bad."

North, Ombric, Bunnymund, and Toothiana were Nightlight's favorite Tall Ones. He understood that they were the "most good." And he understood that they had "knowing," which was his way of calling them wise. Then he thought about Sandman's dream story and the new Tall One—Mother Nature. Was Mother Nature good or bad?

Now that he knew her story, he was not sure. As a child, she had been kind and wild and brave, like Katherine. And like himself. But so much hurt had come to her. So much loss.

It had changed her. And it had changed Pitch.

Nightlight stared at his friends. They seemed changed too. Like they'd lost their knowing and bravery and tallness. Now all they did was "talk the loud," as he referred to arguments, and "do the nothing." This scared Nightlight.

He put his sandy fingertips to his forehead again.

The sand.

Just having it touch his brow made him feel calm and clear. Suddenly, he felt himself understand his friends' behavior. The sand had given him a bit of the "knowing." His friends—they were hurting too. Katherine being gone was hurting them so much that they were scared. Just like he was. And he hated feeling scared. And hated all this hurt. He hated it so much, he couldn't stand it any longer. He thought of the words of Katherine; stories that had washed away when Mr. Qwerty had cried. He could almost hear them from his pocket. It was as if Katherine herself was calling out to him. He had to do something.

He leaped up and slammed his staff on the floor as hard as he could, over and over till the room began to shake. The other Guardians stopped in midargument and looked at him with bewildered awe.

Now that he had their attention, he began to dart about the room in his faster-than-light way, herding them toward the center of the room.

"Hey, squirt," North harrumphed. "Who do you think you are? You can't shove—" Nightlight kicked the Cossack firmly in the rear, moving him along.

"He's gone mad!" said Bunnymund just before Nightlight grabbed him by both ears and yanked him into place.

"Or he's playing some sort of game," mused Ombric as Nightlight jerked his beard firmly and pulled the old wizard along with it.

Toothiana began to see what the boy was up to. She moved to the room's center without any coaxing.

There they stood as Nightlight had insisted, in a sort of circle looking at one another, perplexed and curious about what the boy was up to.

Nightlight now sat cross-legged on the floor in the center of them. He held up Mr. Qwerty and turned the magical book's pages slowly. Then, when he found the right spot, he stood and thrust the book close to each of their faces.

Those four—those magnificent four, the bravest

and most wise of all the Tall Ones who had ever lived, these guardians of the worlds of children—stood sheepishly as a boy (admittedly a magical boy, but still, a mere boy) showed them what Sandman's sand was capable of doing and how to unlock its magic.

Nightlight held his sandy fingertips to his lips and blew. The sand drifted toward them, and as it sprinkled around their eyes and faces, for the second time in twenty-four hours, the four instantly fell asleep. In perfect unison, they teetered, teetered some more, then fell backward onto the floor. They were snoring before they'd landed.

Nightlight again pointed to Mr. Qwerty and said to his napping friends, "Katherine's story! Her life! Her hurts! HER! That's what we save. Remember your knowing. Be stronger than the scared and the hurt, and *dream* a way to save our Katherine!"

Then Nightlight spoke to Mr. Qwerty: "Be writing what just happened on your pages, Mr. Q. That today Nightlight, the boy Guardian, had the knowing of a Tall One."

That's the most Mr. Qwerty, or anyone, had ever heard Nightlight say.

And though Ombric, North, Bunnymund, and Toothiana were away in the land of dreams, they could still hear him. And in their sleepy minds they each were in agreement that what Nightlight had told them was exactly what they needed to hear.

Chapter Eighteen

Do Be Afraid of the Dark

Katherine was surrounded by total darkness. She could see nothing. She couldn't tell if her eyes were open or shut. She tried to blink but wasn't even sure if she'd succeeded—in such darkness, it was impossible to tell. She then attempted to flash her hands back and forth in front of her eyes, but she realized she couldn't move. Her brain was telling them to move, but they didn't budge. And then she realized that nothing would move—not her legs, not her toes, not her smile. She tried to cry out, but nothing happened.

Strangely enough, she didn't feel afraid . . . yet.

Then she began to hear voices . . . low murmurs of speech . . . a little louder than whispers . . . She couldn't make out any of the words. . . . It was just an unnerving babble . . . of wordlike sounds. The voices were deep and menacing . . . mocking . . . as if amused by her being trapped—

It hit her. She was *trapped*. But where? By what?

The voices came closer. She still couldn't grasp what they were saying. But then she recognized a different sound. Crying. It was a girl crying. The other voices were becoming quieter, and she could hear the crying more clearly. . . .

Then Katherine became afraid.

That was her voice crying. But it was the strangest sensation—the crying was somehow separate from herself, as if behind a wall. Then she heard an actual door opening. Light, white with brightness, began to shine in front of her. It was coming from the opening doorway, and she could see the room inside. It was so bright. Almost blinding. Then she began to make out a shape sitting on the floor. It was a girl.

It was her!

But she looked older. *How can this be?* This older Katherine's crying continued. It sounded like a young woman's.

Her clothes were faded and nearly rags. *Why?!*

And in her hands was . . . *Mr. Qwerty! Good!!*

She saw herself start to turn the pages, one by one by one, from the beginning. This Katherine was reading the book very intently, but as she finished a page, a dark hand reached out and tore the pages from the book. She glimpsed her entire history as it was taken away. There was one set of drawings that she could clearly make out. The images she had made for North for his city of the future. She watched her older self close the book and close her eyes. She was going to sleep. She looked unspeakably sad. Tears escaped from her closed eyes.

Then the sounds of the murmuring voices grew louder. . . . They came closer to Katherine, and closer, till it seemed as if they were inches from her . . . just next to her ears . . . They mumbled on and on . . . then began to laugh . . . She could feel breath against her ears and cheeks . . . but she couldn't see . . . Who was it?! What was this awful language? The door—the door allowing the light in—began to slowly close. The bright glow of that other room, the only light, began to vanish. But then she realized it wasn't a door closing, but Pitch himself blocking out the light. He held the pages of her book in his one good hand. He looked at them gleefully and began to laugh.

This is like a nightmare, Katherine thought. And her fear deepened. *This* is *a nightmare,* she realized. Her fear swelled then because she knew—she could *feel* it: She was caught in a nightmare from which she could not awaken.

CHAPTER NINETEEN

A Dream within a Dream . . .

NICHOLAS ST. NORTH DIDN'T realize he was asleep on the floor of Ombric's library in Big Root. The Dreamsand had felled him in midthought, and it was such an odd thought. He was thinking of Nightlight and what in the world the boy was doing. But at the same time he had been briefly distracted by Bunnymund's ears. One of them was definitely longer than the other—by about three-quarters of an inch—then BAM! He was asleep, and while he could still hear Nightlight talking, it was as if the boy were a thousand miles away . . . Something about Katherine . . . about saving her.

And so that's where his mind began to wander as he dreamed—to Katherine. He saw bits and pieces of his time with her. How she had tended his wounds when he was so near death after his fight with Pitch and Bear. How she had brought him out of his bitter, lonely shell. How the two of them had saved each other time and again. Then he dreamed of Nightlight. Of the enchanted friendship between Katherine and the spectral boy.

He was worried, though. Katherine was growing up, but could the same be said of Nightlight? He was an otherworldly creature who never changed; he never grew taller or thinner or fatter—even his hair didn't grow. He'd been a young boy for who knows how long. This was troubling, and then more so as

North's dream began to darken. He saw Katherine becoming older, and growing. Then Nightlight seemed to vanish, to fade away into nothing, and as he did, Katherine's eyes closed. Darkness folded around her like a shroud, a shroud that became Pitch's cape. Then Pitch's face appeared atop the cloak and began to spin faster and faster, making a dreadful sound, a most awful sound, a squealing, screeching, laughing sound. North felt terrified. He felt far away. He felt helpless.

Then, like a bright bolt, everything changed.

Now Katherine was standing over him. Her face was huge. This seemed familiar. . . . It was! It was when North had been turned into a toy by Pitch during the battle at the Himalayas: Katherine had picked him up, held and protected his tiny paralyzed body, and dreamed a dream that had saved him: the dream of his future. The dream had been so glorious. So beautiful. He would build a great city of snow and ice, and it would be filled with magic and good works. It would be like Santoff Claussen, but on a grand, magnificent scale. In bright, brief flashes, he saw Katherine's dreams for him more clearly than he ever had before; he saw it as a reality, of what *could* be: There was a great tower—a polelike spire that rose up from the center of this city—and from this pole, lights would shine out into the world. . . .

And now—now he could clearly hear Katherine's voice urging him to "build this place. . . . It will destroy Pitch. . . . It will save me." Then she said the words they all used, the most powerful words in all of magic: "I believe. I believe I believe."

Believe, indeed! North thought in the wakeful part of his sleeping mind. Katherine was sending him a message from wherever she was being held—he just knew it! It was as strong as any feeling he had ever had. Nightlight had told him to find a way to save Katherine. But he hadn't had to find it. It was being sent to him. By the bond of their friendship, Katherine was telling him how to save her!

He fought now to awaken. But that dratted Dreamsand was so very powerful.

CHAPTER TWENTY

Of Dreams and Relics and Powers Unsuspected

DREAMSAND WAS INDEED POWERFUL, but when the Guardians share an identical dream, the power of their struggle to wake up was even stronger. They had all felt as if Katherine was reaching out to them by sending this dream. So they roused themselves, shaking the sleep from their minds and rising with a cry—a unanimous call to action.

"This dream must be made real! For Katherine's sake and for the good of all," proclaimed Ombric. He felt reenergized. He felt like the Ombric of old. He quickly thought through all the possibilities and circumstances. He nodded to himself as he pondered.

First, this Sandman fellow had gone to help Katherine and insisted they not follow. Now they had their first message from her since she'd been abducted. Ombric nodded once more. Sandman must be making progress. And so the choice was obvious: The city of North's future must be built. Ombric wasn't yet sure why or how, but he knew it would somehow be Katherine's salvation.

He looked up to see his fellow Guardians all nodding along with him, agreeing with the very same thoughts they themselves were having. They all knew what had to be done. It was bold. It was ambitious. It was unlike anything they had ever attempted. A new city had to be built. And an old one changed.

Toothiana flew to the knothole window of Big

Root. "No time can be lost," she called down to the whole village, then she sent out her bright, musical call, singing all the way to Punjam Hy Loo. "The magic elephant must come and help," she added. She called out once more, cocked her head as if listening to the wind, and then, with one flap of her wings, she filled the air around the village with legions of her tiny flying warrior helpers.

Bunnymund tilted one ear appraisingly, then tapped his foot four times on the floor. Within seconds, hundreds of Warrior Eggs popped forth from fresh tunnels surrounding the outer edge of the thick forest around Big Root. They scurried toward Ombric's home on sticklike legs. "The creatures of the air will need help from those of the earth," the Rabbit Man explained wryly.

Ombric took this all in approvingly. He held his

staff aloft. "Guardians!" he boomed out. "Place your relics together, my friends. This mission will require all of our powers!" His owls began to hoot madly, as if they could sense that something unprecedented was about to occur. Bunnymund held his staff against Ombric's, and the jeweled egg on its tip began to glow. Toothiana took out her ruby box and joined it to the staffs. The glow shifted from pale to red, growing ever brighter, glistening. Then they all looked to Nightlight and North. Nightlight motioned for North to go next.

The valiant buccaneer kept his head down; he seemed almost . . . bashful. His voice was barely a whisper when he said, "You are indeed the truest of friends." He paused for a moment, overcome. At last he added, "That you would help make true this dream given to me—"

"My dear North," Bunnymund interrupted. "It is, I believe, a dream we share."

The Pooka's words were true. It was by now a dream that belonged to them all.

North grabbed his sword and swept its crescent-moon tip up to the other relics. The light of North's blade was almost too bright to look into. There was a moment's hesitation.

Ombric said what each of them had suddenly realized. "Will this work without the final relics?" There were five relics from the Golden Age that Tsar Lunar had told them were necessary to defeat Pitch, and they had only three.

Bunnymund's ears suddenly began twitching wildly in opposite directions. Then, just as suddenly, they stopped. "Nightlight!" he yelled. "Your staff! Its powers, combined with the power of Ombric's staff, might be enough . . . if my calculations are correct!"

The others agreed and urged Nightlight closer. But Nightlight resisted—he knew they were wrong. Yet they needed convincing, so he walked up to them and raised his staff up to the other relics. Its diamond tip did indeed begin to glow. The moonbeam that lived inside—his moonbeam, sent by the Man in the Moon himself—flickered and shined brighter than ever. But it was not what was needed. Nightlight could feel the worry and disappointment of his friends as their collective light failed to grow brighter, despite the addition of Nightlight's staff.

"It's still not powerful enough!" Ombric said in a strained voice.

Nightlight felt frustrated. His fellow Guardians were all so knowing, but sometimes they failed to see the most obvious things. Or forgot to look.

Again only Nightlight's childish mind could understand the truth, but if Sandman had been brought to them by Tsar Lunar, then surely he had brought with him something invaluable to the Guardians. *If Sandman was from the Golden Age, then so was his sand.* Nightlight took up a few grains of Sandman's sand and blew it into the light of the relics.

A flash as bright as a dozen suns filled the room instantaneously. At that moment Katherine's dream for North began its journey from the dimension of dreams to the realm of the real.

In the same moment, every other tree in the forest began to uproot itself. Every other creature from Santoff Claussen began to be affected by the magic that was washing through the village. They began to feel that something amazing was about to happen to them.

Half of this wondrous place would make the journey; the other half would stay and hold.

Friends old and new would be separated. But for the good of all.

CHAPTER TWENTY-ONE

Another Nightmare

KATHERINE WAS RUNNING. SHE was in a forest. It was night. There was a bright moon, which made seeing easier, but it also made the shadows even denser and darker in contrast. There was no wind at all; the air lay thick and heavy all around her. There were no insects singing or the usual low commotion of a forest at night. Just an unnerving quiet. The only sound was her footsteps on the grass.

And the sound of the Thing that was pursuing her.

It seemed as though she'd been running for days. Even though she was going as fast as she could, her feet were as heavy as lead. She could barely raise them. She heard the Thing coming behind her. Its movements were smooth and agile. It was coming closer, and quickly.

She had to hurry! Why were her feet so leaden? She seemed to be slower with each step.

She'd glimpsed the Thing, but only for a few fractured instants as it moved from leafy shadows into the moonlight, then back into shadow. Light. Shadow. Light. Shadow. A horrible flickering. Never long enough to see the Thing clearly. It was a squirming, lumpy mass, as big as Bear, but not like a bear at all. Not like anything she could name. It was coiled and knotted, like a tangle of giant snakes, but there was an arm too; a man's arm, Pitch's arm, coming from the Thing's center, clawing at the ground and pulling it forward. Large snaky tails, each as thick as a small tree trunk, twisted out from the main mass, helping the arm move its bulk over rocks and roots with a disturbing ease.

Katherine was desperate to get away from the Thing. She had to go faster. But her feet grew heavier still. Stepping over tree roots grew harder, then almost impossible. The Thing was getting closer.

Ahead was a small clearing where the ground was level. Katherine willed herself to reach it—maybe she could run faster from there. She staggered toward it. The sound of clawing behind her—a lean whisper of slithering—was getting closer. Now she didn't dare look back.

She reached the clearing. Her first dozen steps were a victory; swift and strong, she was gaining speed!

Her feet were light now; she was running! She

could feel the strength surging through her legs as they quickened their pace. She felt revitalized, as if she could run like this forever. Fists tight, she pumped her arms up and down in perfect rhythm with her stride.

Up ahead there was a huge tree. It looked familiar. It was Big Root! Faster! FASTER! If she could just make it to the door, she knew she'd be safe. She tried to call out—someone would hear her, help her.

"Nightlight!" she gasped, but she was too winded. She didn't dare slow down. The Thing was right behind her. It would catch up. She tried again, "Nightlight, help!" But her voice was barely a gasp. Faster. Faster. Faster.

Then her foot came down onto ground that was like mud—softer even. Her leg sank past her knee; her next desperate step went even deeper. She tried to push herself forward, but it was no use. She was sinking.

She could hear the Thing hurrying behind her. She was too afraid to look. She was sinking quickly. She struggled to free herself from the sucking mud, looking yearningly at Big Root all the while. The tree began to pull away from her. How could that be? The distance between them—the ground itself—began to pull up into the air. Were her friends leaving her?

The Thing. She didn't dare turn around, but she knew it was only steps away. As it covered the last bit of distance between them, she heard it reach the mud. It couldn't be more than ten feet away. Five. She closed her eyes. It did no good. She could still see the Thing in her mind. Then she felt the hand of it on her collar.

She tried to scream. But nothing came out. Not even a whimper. If her friends could only hear her, they would come. They always had. Why couldn't they hear her?

Chapter Twenty-Two

At Last a Kind Wind

Sanderson Mansnoozie had been extremely busy. He had scoured the entire planet searching for Katherine with no success.

He had not searched in any conventional manner. He did not prowl about actually looking with his eyes to find her. Nor did he ask people or creatures if they had seen her or noticed anything unusual that might lead him to her. He could have asked any passing cloud about her—he had the ability to communicate to clouds and to other natural phenomena, such as wind and rainbows, but he knew they would not tell him a thing. He'd come to realize they were under the influence of Emily Jane. Of course, they did not know her by that name. They only knew her as Mother Nature. In fact, he was sure they were watching him and reporting to her his every move.

He was not entirely surprised by this. The many tragedies of Mother Nature's previous life had turned her into a solitary and mistrustful being. It wasn't unexpected that she had watchers everywhere. Still, he hoped that if she were being informed of his whereabouts, their old friendship would perhaps spur her to contact him—and hopefully help—but so far no such gesture had come. This did not surprise him either, for even as a girl, she didn't often reach out to others. There were some creatures that were willing to tell him what they knew of how Emily Jane became this nature matriarch.

Sea creatures were more sympathetic to his mission. Especially seashells and mermaids. They had become familiar with Mansnoozie and his island during his long sleep and had watched over him. They saw what had happened when his island had first formed. They'd seen the explosion of his star, and the girl who had been freed by its destruction. They too did not know her as Emily Jane. To them she had no name at all. But they saw the power she had over wind and clouds and natural phenomena. They saw her use the magic she had learned from Typhan. But she remained a mysterious force to them. Always moving. Never resting. Calm one day. Stormy the next.

So Sandy searched for Katherine the best way he knew how: by listening for her dreams.

Nearly every living thing has dreams. Dogs, frogs, gazelles, centipedes, guppies, and certain plants, such as dandelions and weeping willows. Sandman could hear the dreams of every creature—and every person—on Earth. He was certain he had not heard Katherine's. The dreams of the Guardians were distinct from any other dreams he had ever encountered. Not only were their dreams extraordinarily vivid (they had a lifelike clarity unlike any others), but he could also tell that the Guardians had the ability "to dream-share"—their minds could bond while dreaming. But in Katherine's case, that bond had been damaged, and now, perhaps, destroyed. Even creatures as powerful and mysterious as Pitch or Mother Nature had dreams, though Sandy had no clue what those were like; they both had successfully blocked his efforts to read them. But he could still feel the distant presence of their dreams, so he knew they were somewhere.

He also knew North and the others had received a dream from Katherine while he had been searching for her. He had felt their dreams while they experienced this message from Katherine. But he had not *felt* this dream. How could that have been? He was suspicious of Katherine's dream, even though it seemed to be of good intent. How had she sent it? Or *had* she sent it?

For with Katherine, he could feel nothing. Only one thing could stop a person from dreaming, and this was what worried Sanderson Mansnoozie as he sat drifting over the Earth on his cloud of Dreamsand. He was trying to avoid asking the question he most dreaded, but the time had come: Was Katherine no longer alive?

The thought was so dark and sad. Though he had not met this girl, he had heard her dreams many times during his great sleep. So he knew how extraordinary she was.

Could Pitch have been so evil as to end her?

Sandy felt sadness well up inside him, and his cloud of Dreamsand began to drizzle. It was a light rain made of drops of pure sorrow. *That poor girl,* he thought. *As alone and lost as Emily Jane . . . and now perhaps lost forever.*

Dense, dark clouds began to form spontaneously and billow toward him. They were gigantic and storm-like, but they held no wind or thunder. Once Sandman was fully encircled by the storm, he heard a familiar voice bloom around him. It came from the clouds.

"I can stand anyone's tears but yours." It was Emily Jane Pitchiner, now the Queen Mother of Nature! "Besides, I control the rain here. Hold on, I'll send you to the girl."

She will take me to the girl, Mansnoozie thought as relief flooded to even the tiniest grain of sand in his being. *Katherine must be alive!*

He looked up into the cloud nearest to him as it began swirling ever more tightly, narrowing into a sort of tunnel. For the briefest moment, he saw Emily Jane standing at the opening. Her majestic robes whirled around her, and it seemed as though they were what powered the clouds. He felt a deep satisfaction at seeing her at last. She had grown up without his realizing it. Even more gratifying was knowing that his time with her had left some echo of kindness in her soul.

He nodded gravely to her, and she returned the nod. Old friends sometimes need no words to understand each other. Then her winds guided him swiftly up and away, toward Katherine.

CHAPTER TWENTY-THREE

A Dream That Becomes Real

THE COMBINED POWER OF the three relics with the Dreamsand was extraordinary. Their collective energy was nearly nuclear, but smooth and efficient rather than destructive. A quadrillion molecules had been released, all with the intent of instantaneously transporting many of the vast resources of Santoff Claussen to a spot nearly halfway around the planet without damage or upset. Trees from the enchanted forest; books from Ombric's library; the bear; North's elves; dozens of forest creatures of every species, including a small herd of the mighty reindeer; Mr. Qwerty; the robot djinni; Guardians and their helpers—all found themselves in a wondrous frozen landscape.

But there was even more!

From the Lunar Lamadary came dozens of Yetis, the clock that could enable time travel, the magnificent flying tower—accompanied by a note from the Lamas:

May come in handy. Or perhaps useful. Or perhaps necessary. Or even essential. Or not. But perhaps.

Everything arrived and landed at its final destination according to a precise design that had been formulated in North's imagination. North was thunderstruck. He had been working on plans for this "New City to the North," as he called it, ever since Katherine first sent him his dream of the future. But he'd done so alone, during moments of quiet. He'd shown his fellow Guardians a paper model of the city, but that had been a simplistic thing, barely more than a childlike sketch. This . . . this was as if he'd witnessed part of his imagination unfold into reality.

Another reality was that where they had landed was cold. Very cold. They huddled together in a large group, looking around at the icy landscape that surrounded them. They were on a snow-covered peak—miles and miles of snow and glaciers spread before them in every direction. The towering cedar and pine trees from the enchanted forest that had uprooted themselves only a short time ago in Santoff Claussen had been magically replanted around the base of the peak, forming a wall around the city-to-be.

Ombric stroked his beard, cleared his throat, and looked at North inquisitively. His former apprentice had become a wizard of rather astounding accomplishments. And though the old wizard might never admit it aloud, in some ways, North was now more than Ombric's equal.

"Nicely done, my boy," he said. *Now, where exactly are we?*

North could tell that his old teacher was much impressed. In the past he'd have gloated and said something to vex the old man, but he knew this wasn't the time for that. They had the most important mission of their lives ahead of them, and time was short.

North swept his arms wide, as though to include everyone in his response. "We are at the magnetic pole of the northern hemisphere," he called out, loud enough for all to hear. "The first city of the new Golden Age will be here."

"The North Pole," Bunnymund murmured thoughtfully. "I remember when I first magnetized it. Good choice."

Toothiana, her troops, the Warrior Eggs, the Yetis, reindeer, and everyone seemed to agree.

Nightlight just smiled. He was glad to have helped, but he had plans of his own.

CHAPTER TWENTY-FOUR

Something Perhaps Worse

EMILY JANE AND SANDMAN arrived on their clouds at the entrance of a small cave outside the town of Tanglewood in the northeast part of a country called America. The surrounding forests were thick with craggy pine and hemlock, and a great many bats flittered through the trees and in and out of the mouth of the cave. An old, well-worn Indian trail led to the cave, and if Nightlight had been with them, he'd have remembered this dark and mournful place as the spot where Pitch had been frozen for centuries, pinned by Nightlight's diamond dagger embedded in his heart.

Emily Jane enshrouded both herself and Sandman within dense cloud cover so as not to be seen, then said to her old friend, "This is as far as I will go. He is, after all, my father—for good or ill."

Sandy nodded again. He never spoke except through dreams or thoughts. But he understood her reasoning. So he was surprised when she said more, giving voice to her fears.

"He promised me he would not make the girl his princess," she told him, "but he did something perhaps worse."

Sandy frowned.

"You'll see for yourself," she said, knowing Sandy so well, she knew his question without the asking. She took his hand just for an instant. "Be careful. Father is past saving and is now . . . savage, through and through."

Then she turned away hurriedly, her robes swirling around her. Within seconds, her cloud had billowed away into the night sky, taking her with it.

Sanderson Mansnoozie had faced countless dangers in his long and varied life, but this time he felt a fear that was darker than the depths of space.

CHAPTER TWENTY-FIVE

A Place of Endless Possibilities

THOUSANDS OF MILES AWAY at the North Pole, things were progressing with astounding speed and ease. A small but fantastic city was taking shape.

The varied talents of the Guardians and their allies were on full display. The strength of the Yetis, Bear, and the robot djinni had been put to great use in cutting and forming the ice and wood that would make up many of the city's fanciful structures. Toothiana and her tooth fairies zipped in and out of the towers and outer buildings, carving intricately ornate windows and doors through the solid ice walls.

Bunnymund was busy everywhere. From digging out massive blocks of ice to burrowing a network of elaborate tunnels that would connect every building in the city to the rest of the world, he was a blur of city-creating activity.

Ombric and North focused most specifically on the great central tower that would officially mark North's city. The centerpiece for this was the original flying tower of the Lunar Lamadary, and once they had it in place—a tricky maneuver that at

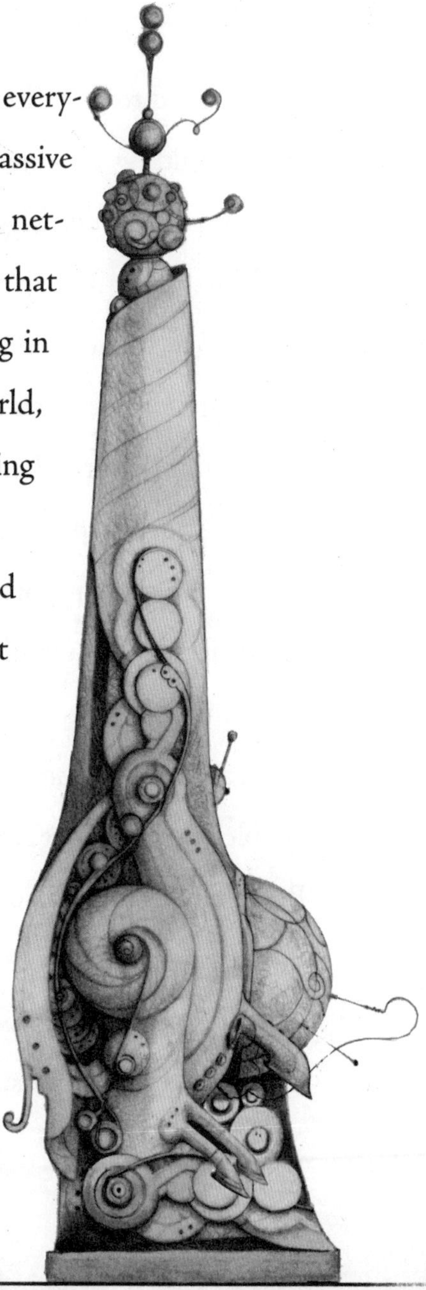

The North Pole

first seemed to defy the laws of gravity—they started in on building an extension to that older structure. They made it taller, bigger, and even more grand.

North had it all planned out: This tower would become a beacon to the world. It would generate a multicolored shimmering of light that could reach almost to the heavens and that he had already named the "northern lights." These lights would be capable of sending forth all sorts of messages to the Guardians and their allies, no matter where on Earth they might be.

Additionally, the tower's precise placement would enable North to see any part of the planet beyond. Best of all, it could also fly. Its transportive power was unlike any that had ever been since the old Golden Age. It could break past the Earth's atmosphere and fly out into the cosmos.

"Think of it, old man," North said to Ombric excitedly. "We will be able to visit the Moon. Meet Tsar Lunar himself! In person!"

Ombric was putting the finishing touches on the new library. All his knowledge, all his wisdom, he was now passing on to this most amazing young man, one whose start had seemed most dubious. The thought made Ombric feel both satisfied and perhaps a little sad. His pupil was now the master. But that's how it should be. He put his hand on North's shoulder.

"The Moon," he said quietly. "After we save Katherine, we'll go meet the Man in the Moon together."

They looked up into the sky. The Moon was just over the horizon. From where they stood, the possibilities were endless.

CHAPTER TWENTY-SIX

A Few Rich Ticks of the Clock

SANDERSON MANSNOOZIE WAS A luminous being. He was infused with shards of starlight, which made him glow rather brightly. This would be a problem if he was to sneak into the dark of Pitch's cave. The bats that clung to the bony tree limbs around the cave's opening noticed him the moment Mother Nature's clouds had left. He was dangerously exposed, and he knew it. The bats fluttered their wings and were about to sing out in alarm, but Sandy was quick. With the flick of one wrist, he sent a fog of Dreamsand that put every bat into a deep and instantaneous sleep. The creatures dropped from the trees by the hundreds, thumping lightly on the ground. There was a quiet hum of snoring bats as Sandy crept into the cave. The strange curling rocks at the mouth of the cave gave way to a long tunnel-like chute.

Sandy spotted something in the shadows, something wispy and dark. He whipped his right hand at it. A bullet of Dreamsand shot toward the thing. There was a light *pff* as the sand hit its mark. Sandy flew down to inspect the target. It looked like a Dream Pirate, only a bit smaller and somehow more vaporous. *One of Pitch's Nightmare Men,* thought Sandy. It was fully asleep and exactly what Sandy needed. He cloaked himself with the nasty, dark creature, completely covering his glow. Now he could proceed unseen.

The inky dark of the cave was nearly total, but

Sanderson Mansnoozie could make out the faintest light emanating from the floor below. He slipped past dozens of Nightmare Men without notice, leaving just enough Dreamsand in his wake to make sure they were put to sleep. This rescue would be difficult, and he needed every advantage in order to succeed.

As he came to the cave's bottom, the light grew only slightly brighter. Mansnoozie was very comfortable with darkness. He'd spent eons in the black of space, and he dwelled most of his time in the land of dreams with his eyes shut. In fact, the only real weakness he had was in staying awake. He could fall asleep with such ease and quickness that on occasion it was a problem. As he peered around the edge of the cave's tunnel and into its main cavern, he felt the telltale twinges of sleepiness starting to lull him. He shook himself awake, not realizing that in just a few more steps he would see something that would jar him awake completely.

He found the source of the cave's only light. It came from a girl, a brown-haired girl who lay sleeping on a coal-colored slab of marble that had been carved into a coffinlike shape. *Katherine! It had to be!* And he could see that she was breathing—she was alive! But what was that around her? He crept closer. She was surrounded by an unearthly glow.

This glow fascinated him. It twisted and spiraled around Katherine like a living thing, and within it, he could see the shifting shapes of tiny Nightmare Men, dozens and dozens of them.

It must be some sort of shield, Sandy thought, feeling a deep unease. Was it to keep her dreams from getting out or to keep nightmares in? Perhaps it was both. Or perhaps it tripped some sort of alarm? He stepped back. He'd thought he knew everything there was to know about dreams, good or bad, but this "shield" had him stumped. He scanned the room. There was no sign of any other Nightmare Men or of Pitch. He was certain the room was empty except for Katherine. So he cautiously lowered his Dream Pirate cloak.

If it's an alarm or a trap, so be it, he decided. *If I act quickly, I can get out of this cave before anyone can nab me.*

And so he crept forward once more.

Looking down at the sleeping girl, he saw that she had a lovely face, but her brow was furrowed, her expression almost tortured.

She's having a nightmare!

Then he looked closer. Small, glowing Nightmare Men were being sucked into her nose and mouth with each breath. His heart began to pound. *She has no*

way of waking! Pitch has doomed her to an eternity of nightmares! Sandy fumed. *The fiend!*

Heedless of potential dangers, he tried to reach through the glowing dome of nightmare light that surrounded Katherine, but his hand was deflected by a painful burst of energy. He snatched his arm back and cradled his blistered hand. He forced himself to keep his mind clear, to not lose his temper. To him, dreams were precious, noble things. Seeing them twisted into something evil was an abomination.

If Sanderson had grown more powerful during his centuries-long sleep, then evidently, so had Pitch. Sandy knew he'd have to be clever and quick to get Katherine from this place. He was certain he'd be discovered at any moment. But how to remove her? Any effort to break through this formidable shield of nightmares would take time and draw attention. Ideas bombarded him, but none were correct, and he was stymied.

He noticed a slight brightening of light behind him. *Pitch has caught me,* he thought, his heart sinking. Still, he spun around and shot streams of Dreamsand from each hand at whatever was sneaking up on him.

The darts of sand were deflected easily. And in the scattered dust Sandy saw not Pitch but Nightlight! Nightlight with his diamond-tipped staff in one hand and a fistful of just-caught Dreamsand in the other. The boy smiled at Sanderson Mansnoozie. Sandy was torn between feeling relief at not being caught and being a little perturbed. He felt he had been quite specific when he'd told the Guardians not to follow him. Still, he couldn't deny he was glad to see this strange, glowing boy. He also was very curious as to why the boy had not been affected by the

Dreamsand. Why had it not put him to sleep?

Nightlight had had an intuition that Mansnoozie might lead him to his Katherine and also that the little fellow might need a bit of help. He'd slipped away from the other Guardians at the North Pole and had been tracking the Dream Captain from a discreet distance, but he knew it was time to take action. Without saying a word, Nightlight leaped forward with his staff and slashed at the base of the coffin-shaped rock upon which Katherine lay. With a single stroke, the diamond-tipped staff cut through the stone completely.

Amazing, Sandy thought, looking on with surprise.

Nightlight enjoyed the little man's astonishment. As did the moonbeam in his staff. But the moonbeam suddenly sense danger. It flashed a warning to

Nightlight. The moonbeam remembered this place well; didn't his boy? The moonbeam had found Pitch here, pinned through his black heart to the very same rock upon which Katherine was now entombed. Pinned by the diamond dagger in which the moonbeam now lived. Nightlight's dagger.

Sanderson turned to the moonbeam, hearing its thoughts. He could see all the details of the memories that flooded through this brave little flash of lunar light.

And as Sanderson Mansnoozie listened, he became sleepy, then sleepier. And in one more blink he was dreaming the moonbeam's memories, about how the moonbeam came to be the light of Nightlight's staff and the amazing story of Nightlight himself.

It all happened in an instant, as thoughts and dreams often do, but what a rich few ticks of the clock this proved to be.

CHAPTER TWENTY-SEVEN

Of Nightlight and Moonbeam and the Power of a Good-Night Kiss

SANDY HEARD THE MEMORIES of the moonbeam exactly as the young light remembered them:

"I was tumbling down like," the moonbeam began. "Into this dark place. I sees things that first time, in the Cave Dark, all Shadowy and nightmare-like. The Cave Dark looks like now, 'cept the Pitch was there. On this same rock. The Nightmare Rock where he was trapped for all that time. That rock must have dust and darkness of the Pitch's hate living ins it still. Trapping Nightlight's Katherine. Making Nightlight's

Katherine dream the nightmares terrible over and over, on and on.

"The thinking of it is a cold horror. I'm remembering the last time. I felt that same cold. When I wents into the diamond dagger. The one that speared through the Pitch, through the Pitch's cold heart and into the stone and held the Pitch prisoner. Kept him so he wasn't alive or dead, just . . . There. All the while, inside the dagger was my boy Nightlight. Surrounded by the coldness awful. For almost longer than ever. It froze my boy. It made him still. And made his memories separate from him. But my light warmed him and wakened him and made my Nightlight boy free. He broke out of the diamond 'cause of me. He needed a bit of the Moon's light to make him strong again.

"But the diamond traps me as it does any

magical light that comes into it. But I'm not minding. 'Cause I know I helps the Nightlight be free. And he should be free. He's the hero of us all. But none really knows the all of his story. Only me. 'Cause his memories stayed here in the diamond. And I can feels them.

"Some knows he was a friend of the Man in the Moon. Some knows about his battling with the Pitch. But only I knows what came before: that Nightlight was the guard of the baby Prince of the Moon. The Nightlight was a special being. The only one there ever was. A boy of light who would live forever and never grow old. And he would always protect the royal young of the Golden Age, especially from nightmares. He would never sleep. And be always watchful.

"But he was doomed to a heartbreak. For though

he cherished and cared for the prince, there would be a sadness time when the prince would become grown and need him no more. And so sorrow would be his life until another child was born to rule, and then the joy and heartbreak would begin again.

"But Nightlight knows this and takes the burden, and every night he stayed and protected the sleep of the prince baby. Every night the Nightlight waited for the Mother Queen and the Father King to come give the kiss good night to their prince. The Magic Kiss of the Good Night. So powerful is this kiss. Takes away all the hurts. Makes the scare and sad go to nothing. My Nightlight has that power too. But he don't know of it. He can't ever give it and stay a nightlight. But his magic is like the parents'. And when they leaves after the kiss, my Nightlight boy says his song:

"'Nightlight, bright light,
Sweet dreams I bestow.
Sleep tight, all night.
Forever I will glow.'

"Then he sprinkles Dreamsand over the prince and watches all the night. Every night. Never to sleep, my Nightlight boy. And he kills any nightmare from the Pitch that could do the princeling harm.

"But then the Pitch so terrible comes, and the Father King and Mother Queen, they know the Pitch will take their boy. To end the Golden Time, the Pitch must do away with the baby prince. So they give Nightlight an oath:

"'Watch over our child,
Guide him safely from the ways of harm. . . .

For he is all that we have, all that we are,

And all that we will ever be.'

"And all around the Pitch is battling terrible, and he captures the Mother Queen and the Father King. And Nightlight hides the prince, but the baby is fearful. The prince baby cries, and this hurts my Nightlight's soul. My Nightlight, he takes the prince baby's tears—he holds 'em tight like treasure next to his heart thumping, and he says the oath, and that makes a magic thing. My Nightlight's hand—the tears burn it, they burn till my boy can't stand it, but he does.

"And then the tears they change; the tears they become strong, the tears they become the diamond dagger. And my Nightlight knows that only he can use this dagger to end the Pitch. My Nightlight knows he will likely die and never see his prince again, so he whispers nice, so nice, to the prince baby, 'Remember me in dreams.' And he flies off to face the terrible, the Pitch.

"And stop him he finally does. And crash here they finally did. And Nightlight felt cold for longer than any should inside that cold heart of the Pitch. He still will never grow up or old, and all the ones he loves will grow past him and leave him, but he must always stay the same. But he 'members almost none of this. Which is my doing. I held on to his memories. So he wouldn't know all his hurts. So he won't be made sorrowful. So me and now you knows of how grand he is in the history of the brave and the good."

CHAPTER TWENTY-EIGHT

Nightlight Has a Memory and the Dreamsand Does Its Stuff

KNOWING THEY NEEDED TO make their escape, Nightlight leaned down to the fresh cut in the stone and opened his fist full of Dreamsand. He held it palm up and blew the sand with one gentle breath. The sand settled quickly into the slice, and once the last little grain had slipped in, the entire block of stone magically lifted a foot or so into the air.

But of course, thought Mansnoozie, having snapped awake as soon as the moonbeam's story had ended, making an instant connection. *Nightlight remembers the powers of Dreamsand, if nothing else.*

Sandy instantly added his own stream of Dreamsand, and soon a sparkling cloud formed under Katherine's stone bed, lifting it even higher. It was time to leave. They were certain to be seen now. Nightlight peered in at Katherine and felt an awful ache. She looked so sad. His beautiful friend was imprisoned in almost the exact same place where he had been. He hated the feelings this brought into his heart.

Sandy let the sand continue to stream forth, its glow brightening the room like sunlight. As Sandy had anticipated, alarms began to sound. The rumble of approaching armies of Nightmare Men and Fearlings rang out from every part of the cave.

Mansnoozie himself wasn't alarmed. He knew that the magic of the Dreamsand cloud was potent. And sure enough, in an instant the three of them flew up and out of the cave and into the evening sky.

They could already see traces of the northern lights of North's faraway tower, showing them the way to safety.

The Nightmare Men tried to follow, but a trail of Dreamsand put all of them to sleep.

Our heroes had made their escape. It had been fairly easy, really.

Pitch was nowhere in sight.

CHAPTER TWENTY-NINE

A Sea of Nightmares and a Helping Hand

KATHERINE WAS ASLEEP AND silent within the energy of the nightmare stone that was now being sped toward the North Pole. She could nonetheless tell that something was happening outside the nightmare world she'd inhabited for . . . days? Weeks? She had no way of knowing. Night, day, twilight—she was oblivious to the real world, for from where she now dwelt, it was always half past terrifying.

At least now she believed she'd been dreaming—that the terrors that hunted her were only nightmares. But they seemed so real. As sharp and true as life. And their fearfulness was just as strong. But something had changed.

In the dream she was now dreaming, she was on an endless and stormy sea. The water was as black as tar and the sky heavy and dim with clouds. She was floating in North's sleigh, but it was rotting in the water and slowly falling to pieces. The waves, huge and coming to mountaintop-like peaks, weren't cresting, but rather each one rose and fell at a continuous roll that was dizzying.

Floating past her were all the people and things she knew and loved: North's horse, Petrov; the giant bear of Santoff Claussen; all her young friends—Petter, Fog, Sascha, and all the Williams—but they were as stiff and lifeless as driftwood. They could not help her, nor she them.

More friends bobbed by: the Spirit of the Forest,

the Warrior Eggs, the owls, the reindeer, then Ombric, North, Bunnymund, Toothiana, and even her beloved Kailash. But not Nightlight. That was her only relief. At least Nightlight had been spared.

Then the dark, murky sky above her flashed and brightened, like an exploding star. She glimpsed a hand, a huge hand. It was visible for only a moment, but she was able to see it distinctly.

Golden colored, it glistened like sand. It was the first bright and hopeful thing she'd seen in all her nightmare journeys. She reached up toward it. It was so close. She lunged and just grazed the tip of one gigantic finger.

Then the hand vanished.

The sky darkened again, and the waves grew even more violent. But now there were dozens of small figures in the water around her. They were quite active, not frozen like the earlier wooden totems of her friends. These were unfamiliar, and they amused her. There were three mice wearing dark-lensed glasses, a dish and a spoon, a leaping cow. All of them happy whimsies, compliments of a friend and ally who knew just what might be needed in this dark place.

So Katherine wasn't fearful as a huge whirlpool began to form, drawing her crumbling sleigh into its swirling vortex. She would be sucked down, surely! The inky spray of the tumultuous sea soaked her and made her cold. So cold. It was Pitch! He was under this awful sea, waiting for her.

But through the dread that now flooded her, something gave her courage. Her hand tingled. The tips of her fingers seemed to glow, as if covered in something barely there. She looked closely. *Is it sand?* she wondered. There were just a few grains—three, four at the most. Then, in a blink, she thought she saw a funny little man who glittered like gold, and she could feel something else . . . Nightlight! Nightlight was near.

As the sea closed around, spiraling her down into its wake, she felt less alone. She knew that somehow, her friends were trying to rescue her. But, oh, the coldness! She could feel that Pitch was so close. She knew that murderous things were afoot.

Chapter Thirty

Meanwhile, Back in Santoff Claussen

EVERYONE IN SANTOFF CLAUSSEN had been a little homesick. Oddly enough they were already home, but half the village was now at the North Pole. So the home half missed the gone half. Petrov, for example, missed his best friend, Bear. They had patrolled the edges of the village together for a very long time. Thankfully, there were others to keep the gallant horse company. Many of the children now rode him on his daily rounds. They had formed their own militia to guard the village. Sascha and Petter were the generals of this young troop. They had enlisted the other children and many of the remaining forest creatures as their captains and lieutenants. No one had a rank below captain, which was one of the fun parts of inventing your own army. The squirrels, chipmunks, beetles, ants, and butterflies all had new military-like uniforms with SC (for "Santoff Claussen") embroidered on their jackets. They had been sent by North himself and had arrived by the train tunnel that now linked Santoff Claussen to his city.

Every few days an Eggomotive train would arrive from the pole, sometimes to bring gifts, news, or returning visitors. The three Williams had just come back and told everyone tantalizing stories of how North's city was growing into the most beautiful place they had ever seen. An enchanted forest now surrounded the city, like the one around Santoff Claussen, but the trees were evergreens—they'd never lose their leaves and all were pointed, like giant cones.

"They are covered with tiny egg-shaped lights, crafted by Bunnymund," explained the youngest William to the others. The city itself sat atop a mountain of ice and snow and was sculpted from the same materials, at least on the outside. Inside, the palatial towers and pavilions, the floors and walls, were grown from sampled hunks of Big Root itself.

On the night of what was now named "the Great Migration," half of Big Root had been transported to the North Pole. But in Santoff Claussen this halving was barely noticeable, for the fantastic tree did not split in half; rather, it divided itself into two trees. Every other limb and root had formed over a new trunk. When the new tree flew away, the original Big Root simply shifted its remaining limbs and roots in a way that made it difficult to imagine that any part of it was gone.

The new Big Root at the pole had then grown itself to take the shapes of all the rooms, stairs, and furniture in North's plans. It was now the only city in history in which every wall, chair, ceiling, and door was alive and able to change upon command.

"If North or Ombric needs a chair, one will come running into place," explained Tall William.

"And North needs a much bigger chair now," added William the Almost Youngest. "He's gotten kinda fat!" They all laughed at the idea.

"The Yetis are great cooks," said Tall William.

"North loves their chocolate and vanilla Moon cookies," blurted William the Absolute Youngest. "White on one side, dark on the other."

"Just like the Moon?" asked Sascha.

"Yep," replied the youngest William. "And *all* good."

"And what of Katherine?" asked Petter.

The Williams glanced at each other. Tall William spoke first. "Ombric received a message just before we left. Sandman found her."

"Is she all right?" asked Sascha.

"We don't know for sure," said Not-as-Old William.

"They are bringing her to the pole," said Tall William.

"What's that?" asked Fog, scratching his head under his SC cap.

"The most magicalist place in the city of North," said William the Absolute Youngest with awe. "Its giant tower in the center of the city—it can do anything. It can even go to the Moon, they say."

That pronouncement drew a collective "wow" from all who listened, even the bugs and squirrels.

Above them, they then saw what looked like a slowly moving shooting star arc across the twilight sky. They looked at it curiously. It was bigger than a star, they realized. It was more like a small cloud. A familiar, slightly sleepy feeling came over them all. Then they knew.

"It's not a star, it's the Sandyman," said the youngest William.

"Yeah. And Nightlight," said Sascha. "They must be traveling with our Katherine!" There was a sudden feeling of hope and excitement among the group.

"Then we must wish them well," said Fog.

So they repeated the words that make all magic possible. The first magic words they had ever learned. The words they hoped would help Katherine.

"I believe, I believe, I believe."

CHAPTER THIRTY-ONE

The Power of the Nightmare Rock

SANDY AND NIGHTLIGHT WERE anxious to get Katherine to safety. Mansnoozie was worried that she had perhaps been trapped inside a nightmare for too long. That she might never recover from such a stream of horror. The black slab of Pitch's Nightmare Rock seemed to be devouring the Dreamsand cloud beneath it; Sandy was using an alarming amount of sand just to keep them flying.

At last they were nearing North's new city. The luminous northern lights ebbed and flowed around them in giant graceful waves. Sandy's fingertips still hurt from his brief attempt to break through the layer of nightmare energy that surrounded Katherine. He paused from spreading Dreamsand to look closely at his aching fingers. The Dreamsand at each tip was scorched with small black bruises that were starting to spread.

He'd never before encountered any nightmare that had had such an effect on his Dreamsand. An odd, sudden urge now compelled him to bring his fingertips to his ear—to listen. And what he heard astounded him. Tiny screaming voices! His Dreamsand was being turned into nightmare sand—each grain of blackening sand now held a nightmare!

As Sandy brought his hand from his ear, staring at the spreading black, thinking of what to do, Nightlight was still watching Katherine. For much of the journey, her sleeping face had been growing ever more peaceful, but now she looked terrified.

The dream cloud beneath them began to lurch and rock unsteadily. Nightlight glanced down. The bright golden sand was churning. Streaks of black began to appear throughout its billowing shape.

Nightlight turned to Sandy, but the little man was already grabbing at him. He jerked the diamond tip of Nightlight's staff to his blackening fingers and began to furiously scrape them. Each scrape peeled the nightmare sand from his fingers; within seconds, his hand was free of the spreading darkness.

But the scraped-away sand began to form into an entity—a small Nightmare Man. And all the sand beneath Nightlight and Sandy was darkening as the dream cloud grew more volatile. They could barely stand as it twisted and jerked, as if fighting for its soul. From both hands, Sandy shot streams of fresh sand into the cloud, but it blackened faster than he could send forth his sand.

They were directly above North's amazing city now, its dazzling lights shining up around them, but they were in desperate trouble.

CHAPTER THIRTY-TWO

Situational Chocolates

DOWN BELOW, THE OTHER Guardians and all the citizens of the new city watched in awe and alarm.

"Just when things seemed to be going so well," said Ombric, rolling up his sleeves and thinking through his list of fighting spells. He wondered if he was still up to the task. *This is for Katherine's sake,* he thought, and strength came roaring back.

"Time to do a little multiplication," said Queen Toothiana, fluttering her wings and clutching her ruby relic.

"Get my sleigh," North said to his elves.

“I believe this situation calls for a particularly potent chocolate,” said Bunnymund. Chocolate had quite an effect on the Pooka. It could transform him in a variety of ways, all of them extraordinary. His ears were already twitching with anticipation.

CHAPTER THIRTY-THREE

Guardian Glory and the Peskiness of Gravity

THE CLOUD ITSELF BEGAN twining around Nightlight's legs and feet, trying to pull him into its blackness. Sandy made long whips of Dreamsand and began to snap them at every coiling tendril, shattering the dark attackers. Nightlight was equally effective with his staff. He stabbed and slashed at the black sand, hacking deep rips and troughs into any shape that threatened.

But the cloud was possessed now. It could change faster than Nightlight and Sandy could manage. It reached out and wrapped itself around that

magnificent pole North was building, sending the rock that Katherine lay upon pitching forward.

Sandy and Nightlight grabbed at the marble slab, trying to steady it, but each touch blasted them backward. The blackened sand beneath them began to change before their eyes; creatures by the hundreds began to form from the dark grains—a cloud of Nightmare Men. They clawed and stabbed at Sandy and Nightlight in numbers impossible to vanquish. The two fought on fiercely, cutting away at the tendrils that were twisting around the pole. But they were simply outmatched by the enemy.

Then, as they were beginning to lose hope, the sky around them filled with able helpers. Queen Toothiana and her warrior fairies. Ten thousand fairies! More! Arrows and swords hitting every mark!

At that point Ombric astrally projected himself

into twenty places at once and obliterated the clouds of Nightmare Men in each place!

And Bunnymund, his mighty ears twirling with the speed of a splitting atom, shot through the air like a bolt of lightning. He'd grown a dozen arms, and each held a sword made of meteor metal.

Then came North on his newly crafted sleigh of his own design, flying at the speed of light and pulled by a team of the Giant Reindeer from the forest of Santoff Claussen.

Together they smashed and blasted through the barrage of Nightmare Men with withering force. The power of the Guardians was awesome to behold.

But the moment of triumph vanished quickly.

The rock that held Katherine slipped through the faltering mass of Nightmare Men and fell with sickening speed toward the ground below.

CHAPTER THIRTY-FOUR

And So They Fell

THERE WAS NO DOUBT that Nightlight was the fastest boy who'd ever lived, but he was not the strongest. As Katherine, on her stone tomb, plunged, Nightlight speared the dense rock with his diamond dagger. Gripping his staff, he used every ounce of his flying strength to try to slow the fall. But not even a hundred Nightlights could have slowed a stone of its mass.

And so they fell.

Precious seconds passed as Nightlight tried desperately to smash his fist through the murky shield of nightmare energy that encased Katherine. At the same time his mind was racing, finding that place where time seems to slow and fate can sometimes lend a hand.

The shield. How to break through?! Can't use the diamond dagger. Could hurt Katherine. How to break? How?!

Bits of Sandy's dream cloud, the grains that had not yet been corrupted, still clung to the Nightmare Rock, stinging Nightlight in the face as they plunged. Several bits peppered his eyes and made him blink. There wasn't time to brush the grains away. They could not make the spectral boy sleep—Nightlight had never slept—instead they made him *remember,* just as the Sandman had predicted.

He remembered so much, so fast, all from his long-ago life with the Man on the Moon. Treasured moments flickered by like leaves in the wind. The oath he had taken, the song he sang every night to the young prince, and the Dreamsand. *Before the Dreamsand! What? What happened before the Dreamsand?* He knew it was important. It could show him how to save Katherine.

It was the most powerful thing of all.

It was stronger than dreams and nightmares, or diamond daggers made of tears, or actions bold and relics ancient.

It was the kiss.

The kiss of the good night. He remembered the Man in the Moon's parents. Every night they'd say good night and kiss the baby. Then he, Nightlight, would bring the Dreamsand to keep the nightmares away. The kiss! It's magic. It takes away all the hurt of the day! At least that's what they'd told him.

Would a kiss from me have any power? he wondered. There was just enough time to try.

Then valiant Nightlight, hero of so many battles, faced the most bewildering moment of his endless boyhood: a kiss.

How is it done?! What do I do? What if I do it wrong?! Something with the lips?! How?!

Just Go! GO!

He closed his eyes and lunged face-first toward Katherine. The nightmare shield gave way like vapor. Its powers only worked against force and fear. And a kiss is neither. It is a hopeful thing. For one eternal instant, Nightlight's lips touched Katherine's, and all of Pitch's dark spells were gone. Her eyes opened. Her tortured sleep was done. The Kiss made everything all right. Katherine was fine. There was no time for even a smile. Nightlight grabbed her hand and flew her away from the plummeting rock. And as it crashed to the ground, he glimpsed a gash in the stone. It was beneath where Katherine had lain. Just under where her heart had been. It was the hole his diamond dagger had left when, so long ago, it had pierced through Pitch and kept them both imprisoned and asleep for ages.

Nightlight felt Katherine's hand in his. He had saved her. And he had saved a part of himself, too—a part that had been forgotten. He had never felt more awake or alive.

CHAPTER THIRTY-FIVE

Growing Up Is an Awfully Big Adventure

WHEN IT LANDED, THE Nightmare Rock had blasted a crater of impressive size at the base of North's city, sending the Nightmare Men retreating. Then Mother Nature swirled up a tempest so strong, it sent them spiraling away and past the horizon. She gave a nod to them all from where she hovered and then flew away before anyone could say a word.

"Mysterious creature," remarked North. Sandy just smiled. He knew that better than anyone.

"One can seldom predict the weather," said Bunnymund. Then they turned their attention to the fallen stone. Though the crater was twenty feet deep and twice as big around, the damaged ground beneath it was made of Big Root wood, so it instantly began to restore itself. As the other Guardians gathered around the disappearing crater's edge, the floor began to level, the slab of black stone rising with it. Since the Nightmare Men had retreated the moment the rock hit the ground, the battle was, for now, over.

"And no sign of Pitch," said North, stroking his beard.

"Not like him at all," Bunnymund added, sheathing his dozen swords.

Toothiana flared her wings. "My human side says 'beware.' My other side says the same, but louder."

"We'll meet whatever comes," said Ombric philosophically. As he gazed up at Katherine and Nightlight, the weariness that had plagued him seemed to pass. Having Katherine back was a tonic to him. To all of them. "For now, let's bask in the victory of friends reunited!"

Hand in hand, Katherine and Nightlight floated down and landed gently beside the rock. The entire city rushed to the site, and there were cheers and instant jubilation. Katherine was safe! North immediately picked her up and hugged her tightly, his laugh now as deep as his waistline was thick.

"You've grown!" bellowed the Cossack.

"So have you." Katherine giggled as she poked her old friend in his now-ample belly.

"The hazards of Yeti cooking," explained Ombric, who joined in the hugging.

The Yetis were clustered nearby. Strangely enough, they were weeping like babies.

"They always do that when they're happy," chirped Mr. Qwerty, who paused from frantically writing everything down in himself so Katherine could read all about it later.

"That is *exceedingly* odd," muttered Bunnymund. "I mean, it's peculiar enough when humans cry, but Abominable Snowmen? That's a bit much."

"Oh, and twelve arms isn't?" countered North.

"I'd have grown one hundred and twenty arms to save Katherine," the rabbit replied curtly, then gave her a dozen simultaneous salutes.

"Is that all, Bunnymund?" asked Toothiana, smiling. "I made thousands of fairies."

The rabbit sniffed and wiggled his whiskers. "Hmm. I hate to say it, but you have a point, Your Highness." His ears twitched like mad. "I'll have to start working on a stronger chocolate. Now, if the ratio of cacao beans to each arm is four to one, then I'd need—"

Bunnymund's calculations were interrupted by Kailash, who waddled up between North and Katherine, honking like mad. Katherine was ecstatic to see her beloved Snow Goose. She hugged the massive bird's neck till Kailash pecked her.

The bustle of conversation was joyous and loud and went on till dusk. Katherine was in awe of North's city glittering around her. She gazed up at the turrets, admiring the exacting carvings and sculptural work, delighting over the colors—red and white stripes—North had chosen. And though Katherine was very happy to see it all—and them all—there was one to whom she very much wanted to speak. She looked through the crowd. Where was he?

But Nightlight knew.

As he brought Sandy through the excited group, Katherine motioned for the little man to come closer. He bowed as he neared her. She smiled at him, and he smiled back. His magnificent, peaceful smile. Though they had never actually met, they knew each other well. They were comrades from the land of sleep and dreams.

The other Guardians began to all talk at once.

"Ah!" said North. "Mansnoozie! At last we actually meet."

"Such remarkable sand," commented Ombric. "I am ashamed I didn't recognize it at once."

"I don't often dream, you know," Bunnymund

told him. "Pookas dream only one night in every thousand years. I do hope you haven't damaged my sleep cycle."

Toothiana smacked one of her wings across Bunnymund's left ear. "You don't have to say *everything* that comes into your head!" she whispered.

"Oh no, not you too," the rabbit said, groaning. "I have to have human lessons from you *and* North?"

But one by one, they all grew quiet. They once again knew what Katherine was thinking. The great link of their friendship had finally been restored. In the silence that surrounded them, Katherine looked at Sandy. He didn't say a word. *He's like Nightlight and me,* she thought. *He doesn't need to say much to be heard. His greatness was in his* doing. *He risked his life to save mine! Is there any greater gift?* She'd not heard his story, but from the other Guardians, she knew: He was one of them. And she knew exactly what was required.

"Kneel," said Katherine to the little man, her voice carrying out over the crowd. "And take this oath." Sandy kneeled before them.

Then they all said the Guardians oath together:

"We will watch over the children of Earth,
Guide them safely from the ways of harm,
Keep happy their hearts, brave their souls,
and rosy their cheeks.
We will guard with our lives their hopes
and dreams,
For they are all that we have, all that we are,
And all that we will ever be."

"From now on," said Katherine, "you will be known as His Nocturnal Magnificence, Sanderson Mansnoozie, Sandman the First, Lord High Protector of Sleep and Dreams, and Guardian to the Children of Earth. Rise, Sandy!"

Sandy rose. *I've traveled to every corner of the universe,* he thought. *But this is where I belong now.* The full Moon shined down upon them. Deafening cheers filled the crystal clear air. Katherine had returned. A great new city had been built. The Guardians were reunited and stronger by one.

The northern lights shimmered out from the North Pole and could be seen all the way to Santoff Claussen.

Nightlight looked out at North's beautiful new city, and for the first time in his ancient life, he felt he was no longer separate from these people he'd called the "Tall Ones" and "Short Ones." He was no longer Nightlight, the boy without a past. Nor was he Nightlight, the boy of endless tomorrows. Tonight he was different. Villains had been vanquished. Spells had been broken. And new spells had been made.

Katherine and Nightlight stood together amid the cheering crowds. Their happiness was linked with everyone else's, but distinct. It was a private happiness that only the closest friendships know when they have weathered a great change. Nightlight took a small pouch from his pocket and gave her the words of the stories that Mr. Qwerty had cried out of her book. He had saved her past and her present. And she his. But his future? That was now like all who grow up: a tantalizing mystery. As the moonbeam had told Sandy, he couldn't use the power of the kiss and stay a Nightlight. Change was coming. Nightlight could feel that. But he was not alone. Katherine once again took his hand.

CHAPTER THIRTY-SIX

Nightlight At Last Sleeps

THE CELEBRATION LASTED TILL very late, long past everyone's bedtime.

Good dreams were had by all. Even Nightlight. For the first time, the boy who never slept finally did. Such dreams! Mansnoozie was amazed by their power.

If only Nightlight hadn't slept.

He'd have been on watch, as he always was before.

He'd have seen Pitch crawl from his Nightmare Rock as it sat in the empty center of the city that was meant to bring about his end.

Pitch's plan was almost complete. He'd read all of Katherine's memories when she was under his nightmare spell. It was he who sent the dream of North's city to them. They had built everything as he had hoped. Unknowingly, the Guardians themselves had smuggled him into the one place he most needed to be. Now he could win this war once and for all. . . .

TURN THE PAGE FOR A SNEAK PEEK

AT THE FINAL CHAPTER IN OUR ONGOING SAGA,

JACK FROST:

THE END BECOMES THE BEGINNING

A Nose Is Nearly Nipped

CHRISTMAS EVE WAS JACK'S favorite day. And for the last century or so he had spent that day in his favorite place.

Jack's tree was the oldest tree in Central Park. A thousand people, maybe more, walked past it every day and had done so for many years, but not one of them knew that Jackson Overland Frost was very often living inside it.

This tree was much older than the park it stood in and was even older than the city of New York itself. It was a sapling when the city was still called New Amsterdam and there were more Native

Americans than settlers living in the swampy forests of Manhattan Island.

By Christmas Eve 1933, millions of people lived within shouting distance of this noble tree, but its secrets were still more absolute than they had been when flintlocks and bows and arrows were the order of the day.

A heavy snow was falling over all of the East. This snow muffled the sounds of the city, though New York was already quieting down. People were done shopping and were heading to their apartments and penthouses and homes. Jack, however, could already feel the thrum of excitement from the children. Sleep, for them, would be difficult. It was, after all, Christmas Eve.

A busy night for Sandman, he thought.

The inside of Jack's tree contained more than a

dozen rooms within its majestic hollow, and the furnishings were a mix of pieces from several centuries. Spears, shields, stools, and pottery from the various tribes of the Iroquois, along with colonial tables and ornate chairs and couches brought over from Europe. There was a tomahawk from the chief of the Algonquians, and the jacket that George Washington had worn the night he crossed the Delaware was hanging on the hat rack that had belonged to Teddy Roosevelt. This tree, like all the tree houses Jack called home, was a handsome, comfortable clutter of the region's history.

He was readying to meet up with the other Guardians when he felt the dull, worrying ache in his left hand. He wanted to ignore it. He knew Nicholas St. North would already be grumping about his being late.

Jack Frost! The fair-weather Guardian! North

would playfully gripe. *Comes and goes when he pleasies!*

The word, my dear North, is "pleases," E. Aster Bunnymund would correct.

Go lay an egg, General Rabbit Bunny, North would retort, and they would begin to amiably argue.

Jack could imagine it exactly. So he grabbed his staff, Twiner, then paused. A sharp pain seared through his left hand. He looked at his palm, at the curious scar etched across it. The inky stain of Pitch's blood had discolored it, and was, Jack knew, the source of the pain, for it only twinged when Pitch or his forces posed a threat.

He turned back to a cabinet, well hidden, where he kept his dagger—the diamond dagger he had made so many years ago from Pitch's tears. He had never finished its construction, but he knew now in his heart that it was finally time. And this worried him deeply.

He took the dagger and tucked it into its sheath. Then he set out for the pole. The North Pole. The thousand or so squirrels that sheltered in his tree were eating nuts and singing squirrel carols around a squirrel version of a Christmas tree, a cone-shaped mound of acorns covered with candles. They squealed "Merry Christmas" to him in squirrel-speak. Jack squealed back to them. He spoke fluent squirrel and chipmunk.

As he leapt out of the hollow in the tree's upper trunk, he felt his hand begin to throb once more. "Not now. Not *tonight*." He gave his hand a shake.

A breeze kicked up suddenly. The trees swayed and lurched; their message clear. Danger was near. Twiner instantly transformed into a bow and quiver full of gnarled arrows.

Jack quickly nocked an arrow.

"Where?" he whispered to the bow.

He let it lead him to where he needed to aim. While Jack could sense danger, Twiner could always see where it was coming from. The wind stilled, and the snow stopped.

"Hmmm. Not only do the trees feel the danger. So does Mother Nature." Jack squinted at the trees around him, spotted something flying through the air toward him.

Nightmare Men! They were coming fast.

But before he could shoot, he heard a telltale sound that made him tense up: the quick, sharp rip of arrows in the air, coming fast. The limbs closest to him shook and bent faster than seemed possible to form a shield. Bark and wood took the heavy hits, and stopping more than two dozen dark arrows in mid-flight. One struck less than half an inch from Jack's forehead.

It was a most unusual arrow: black as coal, with an oily shine. He had not seen an arrow like this since the old days. Since he had been called "Nightlight." He pulled his bow tight and whispered "seek" to his arrow. When he let it fly, it splintered into a multitude of arrows. In the distance he heard a *rat-a-tat* of thuds as each shaft found its mark. Silence followed. Then the snow began to fall again, Mother Nature's signal that the danger has passed by.

He looked more closely at the arrow that had nearly killed him. In the distance he could just barely hear carolers. They were singing "God Rest Ye Merry, Gentlemen." It was one of his favorites.

"Jack Frost nearly had his nose nipped," he said lightly to Twiner. Then he flew off into the night sky toward the North Pole.

He knew for sure. It was time to use his dagger. He

had kept it a secret for so long. Or so he assumed. An attack like this hadn't happened in decades. Jack had made it a priority to be a moving target—impossible to catch. But he could sense a shift; evil was growing. And it could no longer be ignored.

A Less than Early Frost

KATHERINE SAT FIRMLY IN the saddle of Kailash, her giant Himalayan Snow Goose who was perched at the top of the North Pole. Katherine was tensely scanning the busy skies for any sign of Jack. Down below, the Great City of Santa was at the height of its business.

North was bellowing orders from his balcony with a voice amplifier Bunnymund had invented for him. Every citizen of the city who had ears could hear the great man's voice.

"A dream come true for dear North," said

Bunnymund when he had first presented the amplifier to his fellow Guardian. "A nightmare for the rest of us."

But if North was urgent in his orders, he was also jolly.

"Get that shipment of teddy bears sorted properly, or I'll stuff you all with moldy sawdust and putrid hay!" he ordered with a belly laugh to a frantic troop of elves who had arrived with a fresh shipment from the Bear Works building.

North's laugh was of such deep and rumbling mirth that it was rumored to cause earthworms as far away as South America to giggle underground from the tickling sensation it caused. And so, as the last minute preparations for the Great Delivery were being put into place, the North Pole had an air of festive, cheerful panic.

Soon the ten thousand balloon blimps would be launched to their assigned locations across the globe with their resupplies of toys for North's sleigh. An equal number of Bunnymund's underground trains, also loaded with playthings, would steam toward their destinations in many lands.

Of course, sending toys to children across the planet in a single night was a major undertaking, and a certain amount of chaos was to be expected. Yetis were yelling at elves. Elves were shouting at Lunar Lamas. Stuffed animals were nearly at war with toy soldiers. But somehow, with North's urging and good humor, it always seemed to miraculously come together. Every year Katherine was amazed that the scheme worked. *Doing a great kindness to children brings out the best in every creature,* she thought. But where was Jack tonight? She slid off Kailash's back

restlessly. She always knew when he was in trouble. And tonight the trouble she sensed was deep. Jack was not just in trouble. Her boy was in great danger.